FIRST MEETING

I noticed a boy about sixteen or seventeen crossing the street toward my Dad's building. He must have felt my nervous presence hovering above him because he turned and looked up at me.

"You live here?" He had straight hair sort of parted in the middle, and a long serious face. His skin was tanned and smooth.

"I'm visiting my father."

A slow smile spread across his face. "Oh, where are y'all from?" he said in a mock southern accent.

My face flushed. "North Carolina."

"What's your name?" he said.

I didn't want to tell him my name. If he thought my accent was funny, he'd die when he heard my name.

"You haven't got a name?" he said.

"It's Blue," I said softly.

He nodded as if he weren't surprised at all. "Blue—like your eyes."

I smiled a little. "Yes."

He kept staring at me with a thoughtful, sexy expression. I wondered if I was more appealing to New York boys than North Carolina boys. I cleared my throat and said, "What's your name?"

"Nathaniel."

What a beautiful name, I thought. But I just nodded. I didn't trust my voice.

**Other Scholastic Paperbacks
you will enjoy:**

Dear Lovey Hart, I Am Desperate
   by Ellen Conford

Do You Love Me, Harvey Burns?
   by Jean Marzollo

Flunking Out
   by W.E. Butterworth

Girl Meets Boy
   by Hila Colman

Halfway Down Paddy Lane
   by Jean Marzollo

Hello...Wrong Number
   by Marilyn Sachs

If This Is Love, I'll Take Spaghetti
   by Ellen Conford

Just the Two of Us
   by Hila Colman

Sweet Friday Island
   by Theodore Taylor

When We First Met
   by Norma Fox Mazer

Love Always, Blue

Mary Pope Osborne

SCHOLASTIC INC.
New York Toronto London Auckland Sydney Tokyo

ISBN 0-590-33216-3

Copyright © 1983 by Mary Pope Osborne. All rights reserved. Published by Scholastic Inc., 730 Broadway, New York, NY 10003, by arrangement with Dial Books for Young Readers, a division of E.P. Dutton, Inc.

12 11 10 9 8 7 6 5 4 3 2 1   10   4 5 6 7 8 9/8

To my mother and father

---

and with thanks to Will again

Love
Always,
Blue

1

I gave up studying for my exams around six o'clock and lay back on my bed. Mom still wasn't back from the club, so the house was quiet. My room was gray and shadowy—thick clumps of leaves scraped against my screens, crowding out the June sunlight.

I wondered if my dad would call me from New York tonight to wish me happy birthday. I imagined what it would be like to sit with him in the back of an empty theater up there while actors rehearsed one of his plays onstage. I pictured what I might wear— maybe a gauzy yellow dress or a sailor blouse with a pair of faded jeans.

I raised my bare foot in the air and propped it against my bedpost. What a big foot to be coming from such a skinny leg, I thought. I rolled over onto my side, trying not to worry about my body, trying to get back to my theater dreams.

The phone rang. I jumped and grabbed the receiver beside the bed and said, "Hello!"

"Hey there." It wasn't him—it was Susan, my best

friend for the last two years. "What's happening?" she said.

"Hi, Susan. I thought you had a date."

"Well, you're not going to believe this," she said, "but Wayne dropped his Walkman on his foot and he broke two toes!" She shrieked with laughter.

"You're kidding. When did this happen?"

"In sixth-period study hall! He was trying to hide it from Mr. Tate and he dropped it and he was wearing sandals and he yelled bloody murder and had to go to the infirmary! Clayburn helped him get there. I'd like to died when I heard about it! It's just like Wayne. It was his middle toe and his baby toe!" She cracked up again.

I had to laugh too. I couldn't help liking her, even though she wasn't very intellectual. She didn't read at all, but she had a great sense of humor and she seemed to admire me a lot. She thought I was an "artist type" and everybody would "hear from me" someday. "So what are y'all doing?" she said after she'd stopped cackling.

"You mean me and my mother?"

"No, just you."

"Then don't say 'y'all'—that's short for 'you all,' which should be 'all of you,' which is obviously more than one person." I had told her this many times.

"You're still trying to make a Yankee out of me," she said. "But you better just 'fer-git' it!"

"You're hopeless," I said.

"It's the truth," she said. "Hey—you want to go to Hardee's?"

"Now?"

"Yeah."

"No, thanks."

"Oh, come on, girl. Don't be pitiful. I won't desert you like I did last time. But you'd have deserted me too if Malcolm Lowe had asked you to drive around with him."

"I don't care if you desert me," I said. "I just don't want to sit around and listen to a lot of dumbheads grunt about cars and beer and breasts."

Susan cackled again. "That's hilarious!" she said. "You ought to be a writer, Blue. I mean it. Come on—maybe you'll meet the Yankee of your dreams there. Maybe he'll be wearing an artist beanie and driving a little black Triumph." She laughed again.

"You're the one that's pitiful," I said.

"Come on and go—I'd love to be out having a good time while Wayne sits home with two broken toes. Please . . ."

"Well . . . what are you going to wear?"

I heard a sharp intake of breath. "My—new—all—cotton—L. L. Bean sweater!" If she'd announced she was going to marry Bruce Springsteen, she wouldn't have sounded more impressed with herself. "And what about you, girl?" she said.

"My—old—green—Hanes—T-shirt!" I said.

She screamed. "Meet you there in twenty minutes?"

"Oh, okay."

"Great. I have to get ready now and admire myself for a while," she said. "See you there."

"Now don't you be late," I warned her. "I hate standing there by myself trying to look nonchalant. I hate it—do you understand?"

"Yeah, yeah. I know how sensitive you are. I'll rush there and protect you from any talk about breasts."

"Get out of here," I said. " 'Bye."

It was cloudy when I stepped out the front door onto our columned porch. The sky was steely gray and the air smelled like cut grass. As I headed toward the highway, I could feel my jeans brushing against my ankles. I couldn't believe it—my jeans always seemed fine when I put them on and then later they seemed shorter. I leaned down and yanked on them a couple of times. I hated short jeans—I felt like Olive Oyl in short jeans.

There were lots of parked cars when I got to Hardee's but no sign of Susan; so I walked quickly to one of the empty cement tables and sat down. I watched the road for her, trying to ignore all the boys leaning against their cars, talking and laughing loudly.

When I finally saw Susan enter the parking lot, I stood up and waved. But she didn't see me. A blond guy leaning against a Volkswagen said something to her and she stopped.

I swore under my breath. I felt like a fool, standing up in full view of everyone. I shouted, "Susan!" but she still didn't notice me. I hurried across the parking lot to her.

"Oh hey, Blue," she said. Then she looked back at the blond guy and said, "What were you saying?"

"You want to get in and sit for a while?" He nodded toward the backseat of the VW he was leaning against.

"Well, we were going to get a Coke," she said.

He seemed to notice me for the first time. "Oh. Well, why don't y'all get your Cokes, then come on back and join me and Mike." The driver of the VW was sitting at the wheel of the car, staring coolly out the front window. He was handsome with bony cheeks and dark shiny hair.

"Sure," Susan said. "Come on, Blue. Don't y'all go away," she called back to the blond guy.

"They're seniors," she hissed as we headed into Hardee's. "On the football team. I don't believe it. I don't believe it—"

"The driver too?" I said.

"Yes, both of them!" she said, her eyes wide. She ordered us two Cokes and some french fries for herself. "I have to have fries when I'm this nervous," she said. "They help calm me down." She shook her head from side to side and sucked air through her braces. "His name's Tony Bradshaw—my guy. Your guy's Mike Ewell. Tony and Mike. Tony and Mike."

I was starting to feel hysterical too. My guy was Mike. By the end of the night would the whole parking lot think of Mike as "my guy"? I'd never been out with a football player. Hell, I'd never even car dated.

"Come on," Susan said. She held her french fries

in one hand and her Coke in the other and led us out of the restaurant.

"I don't know what to say," I said frantically, knowing I wasn't going to get much advice in the fifteen seconds it would take to get to their car.

"Just act cool," she said. "Act cool. Be friendly."

Tony, the blond guy, was still leaning against the car when we got there. He tapped Mike's elbow.

"What, man?" Mike said, sounding irritated. He glanced from Tony to Susan and then to me.

"These young ladies are going to join us for a little bit," Tony said. He put his hand on Susan's shoulder. Mike looked at me without smiling. He got out and let Susan and Tony into the backseat. I walked around and climbed in front.

Mike got back in the car and stared at me. He reminded me a little of John Travolta. I smiled at him, then looked away. When I looked back at him, he was still staring.

"How are y'all doin' tonight?" he said.

"Fine."

He nodded.

Susan and Tony were laughing about something in the backseat. Mike glanced at them. I sipped my Coke and desperately tried to think of something interesting to say.

"What's your name?" Mike asked me.

"Blue."

"*Blue?*"

I nodded.

He laughed and turned to Tony. "Hey—her

name's Blue," he said. But Tony didn't hear him. He was still laughing about something with Susan.

Mike shook his head and looked back at me. "Where did you get a name like that?" he said.

"It was my grandmother's maiden name."

"Oh, far out. So—what are you doing this summer, Blue?" he said.

"Well, I'm not sure," I said. Then I surprised myself by saying, "I might be going to New York City."

"Whoa—the Big Apple. Far out."

Susan and Tony were laughing harder now. Mike looked back at them. "Hey, y'all better straighten up back there," he said, grinning. He looked back at me. "What do you want to go to New York for?" he said.

"My father lives there. He's a playwright. He lives in Greenwich Village."

"He does?"

"Yeah. Have you been to Greenwich Village?"

Mike shook his head, then he looked back at Susan and Tony again. "Hey—what are y'all laughing about?" he said.

"She flipped a french fry in my face," Tony said, laughing.

"What did you want to do that for?" Mike asked Susan.

"Well—he looked like he needed to get a french fry in the face," Susan said.

That broke Mike up. He turned halfway around in his seat and said, "Where did you learn to flip fries, girl?"

This led to a conversation among the three of them about how far you could flip a french fry. After that they discussed how much gas mileage Mike's VW got, and then they fought over the merits of Myrtle Beach versus Wrightsville Beach.

I acted like I was interested in what they were talking about, but all the time I felt humiliated. Mike didn't care about what I was doing this summer, or anything else about me.

I started thinking about my dad. He wouldn't fit in with these guys either, I thought. He would think they were boring. I thought they were boring too—even if they were football players and seniors.

I wanted to go home and be by myself. "Well, I better be going," I said casually.

No one seemed to hear me. Susan was giggling while Tony and Mike argued over who had drunk the most beer at Wrightsville Beach during the Azalea Festival. "I have to go," I said, suddenly desperate. I opened my door.

Susan leaned forward. "Oh, Blue, you don't want to leave now, do you?" she said.

"I have to. I told my mother I'd be back soon," I said as I got out of the car. "I'll see y'all later." I waved, and Tony and Mike waved back.

I closed the car door and headed quickly out of the parking lot. It was starting to get dark as I walked along the highway; car lights bore down on me, whished by, and vanished. I remembered how I used to rush home, feeling breathless and afraid, then see my dad's car and feel safe for another day. Months

before he actually left, he told me that he and my
mother might split up. I appreciated him confiding
in me, but I started acting crazy after he told me
that. I raced home from school every day, afraid he
might have gone. I grew so afraid, I stopped going
out with Susan and my other friends. I never spent
the night with them. I thought if I took my eyes off
Dad for long, he'd slip away.

But it didn't matter. When he'd left last February,
I'd been watching. And even though I'd screamed
for him, he hadn't stopped. When he'd gone out
to his car, I'd run out in the cold dark and tried to
hold on to him. He'd said, "No, don't," his voice
breaking. Then he'd gotten into his car and driven
off.

I charged across the highway and started up the
hill to our neighborhood. I imagined my dad's red
Chevette parked in our driveway. Maybe he'd driven
down for my birthday. Of course I knew he hadn't,
but what if he had?

I walked under the dark trees that lined the sidewalk of our street. I imagined him standing there
under the porch light. I wished I wasn't so sweaty
in my T-shirt. Maybe before he saw me, I could
sneak around to the back door so I could go inside
and clean up a little.

I nearly laughed out loud at myself, but my heart
was beating hard as I neared our house. I hurried
past the Burdocks' lawn, then halted behind a giant
holly bush at the edge of our yard and looked around
it.

He wasn't there. Of course not. There was no red Chevette in the driveway—just the ragged shadow of our dogwood tree.

2

The screen door closed behind me with a slam.

"Blue?" Mom said. She was calling from the TV room.

"What?"

"Come here."

I walked through the lamplit hall and dark living room till I stood in the doorway of the TV room. Mom was sitting on the flowered sofa with a bare foot tucked under her as she read the paper. Kermit the frog and Anne Murray were singing a duet on TV. "What?" I said.

"Where were you?"

"Hardee's. I went with Susan to get a Coke. She's still there." I turned to go.

"Oh . . . I put a frozen lasagna in the oven for us," Mom said.

"Thanks, but I'm not hungry now. Maybe later." I went back through the dark living room to the hall.

"Blue?"

"What?" I called from the stairs.

"Where are you going?"

"Up to my room to study."

"But it's Friday."

"I know. I have exams next week."

I tramped up the stairs and crossed the hallway to my room. I found my way over to my bed without turning on the light and lay down on my stomach. I listened to the crickets outside. This house was so huge and empty. I felt as if my mother were miles away, listening to the Muppets on a sunny little island.

Mom had inherited the house and lots of money when my grandmother had died two years ago. I'd always thought that had been the beginning of the end. It seemed to me Mom and Dad had been more alike when we'd lived in Chapel Hill. On weeknights and weekends, Dad had worked on his plays. And Mom had even been in some community theater productions at night. I'd seen her in *Night of the Iguana* when I was nine.

"Blue?" My mother's voice came from the dark hall.

"What?" I said, half sitting up.

"What are you doing in the dark?"

"Nothing. Just listening to the crickets."

"Listening to the crickets?"

"Yeah. They sound like castanets."

"Can I turn your light on?" she said.

"Yes."

I heard her bare feet pad across my floor. Then she turned on my lamp. She stood in the lamplight, her black hair falling over her shoulders. In her green sundress she looked like a pretty country girl. "It's sad, honey, finding you in the dark," she said. "It's only eight thirty."

"I'm okay. Did you know that crickets have a way of throwing their voices? That if we went outside and tried to find them by just following those castanet sounds, we wouldn't be able to?"

"I didn't know that. Why didn't you stay out with Susan? You could have called if you'd wanted to stay at Hardee's longer."

"I didn't want to."

"Why not?"

"I always have a terrible time at places like that."

"Why, honey?" She walked over to me and sat on the edge of the bed.

I stared at the ceiling. "Because I don't fit in. I don't know what to say, and when I say something that's important to me, no one listens. Everyone drifts away from me, and I end up feeling lonelier than if I were just here by myself."

"Do you like any of the boys you meet when you're with Susan?"

"Sometimes I think there's a possibility I might like them. Tonight I was paired off with this guy who looked a little like John Travolta."

"What happened?"

"Well, first he thought my name was hilarious, and then he stopped listening to me altogether. He proved to have a brain about the size of a pea."

She laughed. "I'm amazed that he wasn't interested in you," she said.

"Boy, I'm not." I sat up. "One thing I want to

know is—why do you think my jeans get shorter between the time I put them on and the time I walk down the street?"

"What are you talking about?"

"My blue jeans get shorter as I'm wearing them!"

"I think that's scientifically impossible."

"My jeans defy modern science." I lay back on my bed. "Or else I'm growing taller every minute."

"What's wrong with being tall?"

"Nothing. Except it contributes to my overall general feeling of being ugly."

"Ugly? Are you kidding?" she said. "Madge Howell told me the other day you were lovely. She said you reminded her of Audrey Hepburn."

"Who's she?"

"Remember that movie we saw on TV that you liked so much—*Breakfast at Tiffany's*?"

"Oh—that girl."

"Yes, her. She's lovely."

"Well, if I'm so lovely, why do boys act irritated when they find out they're being paired off with me?"

"I don't know," she said. "Maybe you make them nervous."

"Ha!"

"Well, maybe you do. What do you say to them?"

"Nothing. I don't know what to say."

"Well, what did you talk to John Travolta about tonight?"

"What did I talk to him about?" I stared at her for a few seconds, knowing I was about to head into trouble. "Well, I told him I might be going to New York this summer to be with Dad"—I went on without giving her a chance to react—"but in the middle of telling him about it, he just turned away and asked Susan and her date what they were laughing about."

Mom didn't say anything.

"What's wrong?" I said.

"What makes you think you might be going to New York this summer?" she said quietly.

"Well, I have to go sometime."

She kept staring at me. It was as if an air raid siren had just started to sound in the distance, and she was trying to decide whether or not to ignore it. She looked away, reached behind her neck, and held her hair up for a few seconds as if she were hot. "Well, one thing's for sure," she said. "I'm getting hungry. You sure you don't want any lasagna?"

"No, thanks."

"Are we still going shopping in the morning for your birthday?" she said.

"Sure."

She nodded, then stood up. I watched her as she picked a blouse up off the floor and draped it over the back of a chair. I felt that beneath the surface of our behavior, a battle was starting—lines were being drawn, people were running for cover.

She looked at me. "Why don't you try to get most of your studying done tonight—so we can spend the whole day together tomorrow?" she said.

"I don't really have much more to study," I said.

"Good—then come down and watch *Dallas* with

me later." She avoided my eyes as if she were afraid that any second I might jump up, throw back the covers, and make her look at the battlefield.

But I just stared at her, not moving a muscle.

"Okay?" she said.

"No . . . I think I'll probably go to bed early."

"Okay, honey. Good night." She smiled, then turned and escaped from my room.

3

I woke up early the next morning. I got out of bed and went into the bathroom and splashed water on my face. Then I pulled a comb through my long brown hair. I knew it was silly, but I wanted to look nice when I talked to my dad.

I went back into my room, sat down on my bed, and placed the phone on top of my pillow. I dialed slowly. The phone rang once and then again. On the third ring he answered.

"Dad?" I said.

"Blue?"

"Yes." I laughed breathlessly. "How are you doing? I was just wondering how you were."

"I'm okay, babe." He sounded half asleep.

"Guess what? It's my birthday," I said.

"Oh, wow. I forgot. I'm sorry."

"That's okay. It's no big deal. I just thought I'd call you."

"Oh no—I'm sorry. I love you, bluebird. I'm an idiot for forgetting."

"That's okay."

"I've missed you a lot lately, bird," he said.

"I've missed you, too." I could feel my throat starting to close up.

He didn't say anything for a second. "So, are you fifteen today or what?" he said.

"No, thirty-two."

He laughed. "What are you going to do to celebrate?"

"Mom and I are going shopping, and then maybe go to a movie or something."

"That sounds nice."

"I wish you were going to be with us."

"Hmm."

"Well, what are you going to do today?" I said.

"Not much. Oh, but hey—guess what—they're doing a reading of my play tonight."

"Who is? What play?"

"My new one—the one I was working on all winter. A guy I met in a bar is a director, and he's having a reading at his loft tonight. If it goes well, he might do it as a showcase."

"What's that?" I said.

"It's off-off-Broadway."

"Off-off-Broadway! Dad, that's wonderful!"

"No, it's not that big a deal."

"It is too! It's wonderful! This can be my birthday present."

"I wish I could give you a better present than that."

"This is the best present in the world. . . ." I dug

my nails into my palm. "Dad, do you think if your play gets done, I could visit you soon?"

I heard him take a deep breath. "Blue, if this play gets done, I'll really really want you to come up here and visit me," he said.

"Okay," I said softly.

"You think Mackie would let you?"

"Well, last night I told her I'd been thinking lately about going to see you sometime, and she didn't say no."

"Well look, don't mention any of this to her yet, okay? Let's wait and see what happens with the reading."

"Okay."

We were both quiet for a moment. "Well, happy birthday," he said. "I love you."

"I love you, too." I didn't want us to hang up. "Is anything else new?" I said.

"No, I guess that's about it."

"Well, let me know how the reading goes."

"Sure."

"Thanks."

"Happy birthday. I love you," he said again.

"I love you, Dad. 'Bye."

"Good-bye, bluebird."

I hung up the receiver and stared at it for a moment. Every time I talked to him on the phone, I missed him unbearably. I wished I could charge downstairs right now and announce that his play might be done in New York—off-off-Broadway; and that he'd actually said he'd want me to come visit him when it was done. But I felt like he and I had a secret plan now, that I really shouldn't badger Mom till I'd heard from him again.

When I got down to the kitchen, Mom was in her yellow robe, sitting at the table, drinking coffee and reading the paper. "Morning," she said. She eyed me cautiously. "Happy birthday."

"Happy birthday to you!"

"You sound like you're in a good mood," she said.

"You would be too if you'd just survived being fourteen."

She laughed. "But now you have to endure all of fifteen."

"It'll be better. I'm sure of it." I drank some juice, looking at her over the rim of my glass. "I can feel it in my bones," I said.

"I'm glad to hear that," she said.

"Yep." I put my glass down and smiled at her.

"Do you know something I don't know?" she said.

"No, no. Hey, didn't you say we were going shopping first thing? You better get ready!"

"Okay, okay," she said, closing her paper. "Just give me a minute to get dressed."

"I'll wait for you out on the porch," I said.

The sun felt warm on my arms as I leaned against a porch column and watched the little kids across the street playing. They were rumbling up and down their driveway on plastic motorcycles. I started thinking about being in New York with my dad, sitting in the theater on opening night of his play.

"Let's go," Mom said. She stepped out of the

house wearing designer jeans and a red polo shirt.
"What a glorious day," she said.

"Oh, it is, it is, it's just . . . glorious," I said,
grinning at her.

"Now don't you tease me," she said, smiling.

We got into the car and I buckled my seat belt as
she started up the engine. "Do your seat belt," I
commanded her.

"Okey-dokey."

"Okey-dokey?"

"Hey"—she pointed her finger at me—"stop that."

"If I don't—are you going to give me a 'knuckle
sandwich'?" I giggled. "You should really work on
getting rid of your clichés, Mom."

"And you should work on respecting your elders,
smartie," she said as she pulled out of our driveway.

"Smartie!" I screamed. "You're hopeless!"

"Blue, stop!" she said laughing. "I can't talk to
you. Now—do you want to go to the mall or downtown?"

"Downtown, of course. I simply can't tolerate the
Muzak at the mall!" I started singing in a mocking
voice: " 'Cause honey, I miss you. . . .' "

"You're a live wire today."

"A live wire?"

"Okay, okay!" she yelled. "Quit!"

"Okey-dokey!" I said.

"Blue!"

We both laughed, then Mom looked at me and
said, "It's nice when you act this way. It's like you
have your old personality back."

I stared out the front window. I guessed my old

personality had left me this past winter. Now and then it came back briefly—but just for a morning or an afternoon. My personality was like a mayfly, I thought. I'd read in an Edwin Way Teale book that once they hatched, mayflies only lived for an afternoon. Lately I'd been collecting odd facts about insects. Along with my mayfly fact, I'd recently written down that a bee's wings moved 180 to 250 times a second.

"What are you thinking?" Mom said. She sounded worried—as if she were afraid I'd just lost my personality again.

"About bees' wings."

"What's that?"

"Bees' wings."

"Is that something you wear?"

I looked at her. "Yes. It's a kind of shoe."

"Do you want them for your birthday?"

I cracked up. "No, Mom! *Bees' wings*—the wings"—I flapped my arms—"of bees!" I buzzed my finger through the air.

She tilted her head as she looked at me. "Blue, you're so strange," she said.

We parked behind Thalhimer's and went in through the back entrance of the store. "Well," Mom said, "what should we buy you—a bathing suit? Shorts?"

"No. I'm not wearing shorts this year."

"Why not?"

"Because I have long thin sticks for arms and legs."

"Oh, don't be silly—look, aren't those pants adorable?" She pointed to a display of painter's pants in pastel colors.

"They're not 'adorable,' but they're not bad," I said.

I tried on a pair of yellow painter's pants with a bright-green T-shirt. Mom watched me as I stood in front of a three-way mirror. The pants were real long—they completely covered the tops of my sneakers. I held my hair up as I studied myself.

"Gee—that looks good," Mom said. "I like your hair like that."

"What, like this?"

"Yeah, wait—wait—I have some bobby pins." She dug in her purse. "Move your hands," she said. She stuck some pins in one side of my hair, then moved around me and pinned up the other side. "There!" she said. "Now you really do look like Audrey Hepburn."

I could see it a little. My neck was long and thin. I stood up straighter.

"You look so much more attractive when you put your shoulders back," Mom said.

"Okay, okay. No posture nagging on my birthday."

"Sorry, I forgot. Well, what do you think about the outfit?"

"I really do kind of like it."

"Good—happy birthday!"

"Thanks, Mom."

"You want to wear it now?" she said.

"Yes," I said. "I'll get my things." I got my clothes

from the dressing room and joined Mom at the register.

"Gosh, I like your hair like that," she said. She handed her credit card to the saleswoman. "Now, you want to have a nice lunch somewhere?"

"Sure."

"Would you like to go to the club? Or is that a terrible idea?"

"No, it's fine," I said.

"They have a pretty good lunch in the Players' Lounge," Mom said. "It's not as snobby as the main dining room."

"Don't worry. It sounds nice," I said. I was having a good time with her. I didn't want us to get into our usual skirmish about the club. Mom had joined it the week after Dad had left. Uncle Walter had gotten her in.

"Thank you, ma'am," Mom said as she took her credit card back from the saleswoman. "What else would you like for your birthday?" she said. "A couple of short skirts?"

"No way—they'll expose my skinny legs."

"Oh, Blue, I'm going to skin you alive," she said.

"Skin me alive? Mom—that's disgusting."

4

Mom parked in the club parking lot, then quickly brushed her hair and put on some lipstick.

"You look glorious," I said as we got out of the car. "You'll be in the Layette social column tomorrow—'Lovely Mackie Murray was seen at the country club Saturday . . .' "

" 'And she was accompanied by her daughter, Blue Murray, who's certifiably insane,' " Mom said.

We climbed the steps to the plantationlike building. I glanced at a few women sitting in deck chairs on the veranda.

"Mackie!" one of them shouted. She had a blond ponytail and was wearing a little tennis outfit.

"Hi, Lou," Mom said, waving.

Lou jumped up and started toward us. I turned to Mom. "She looks like a Barbie doll," I whispered.

"Shhh," Mom said, smiling.

"How are y'all doing?" Lou said in a baby-like voice.

"Fine," Mom said. "You haven't met my daughter, have you? Lou McGovern, this is Blue."

"No!" Lou exclaimed with exaggerated enthusiasm. "Hi, Blue! What a *pleasure* to meet you!"

"Hi." I turned to Mom, expecting her to smile or wink at me, but she was looking at Lou.

"It's Blue's birthday," Mom said.

"My goodness!" shrieked Lou. "Happy birthday, Blue! That's marvelous!" She grinned at me like a half-wit. I glanced quickly at Mom, trying to radio to her that I thought Lou was hilarious—didn't she? But Mom just looked a little uncomfortable. "Well, I think Blue and I are going to head in," she said.

"Oh, are y'all going to eat?"

"Yes—just a quick lunch."

"Well, maybe I'll join you. Let me run tell Sally—hold on." She hurried over to one of the women on the porch, her ponytail bobbing up and down.

"Is she going to eat with us?" I said unbelievingly to Mom.

"It sounds that way." Mom looked bothered too. Neither of us said anything as we watched Lou gush something to her friend, then head back to us. "All set!" she said.

"Oh, good," Mom said.

Lou walked ahead of us into the Players' Lounge. "Over there?" she said, pointing to a table next to a bay window that overlooked the golf course.

"Fine," Mom said. We went to the table, and Mom and I sat down.

"Y'all sit tight," Lou said. "I'll get us something from the bar. The little gals here take forever. What do you want, Mack? I'm having a piña colada."

"A gin and tonic's fine for me," Mom said.

"And what can I get for you, birthday girl?" Lou grinned at me.

"Nothing, thank you."

"You sure?"

"Yes."

"All righty. Back in a jiffy," she said, and she bounced away from us.

"Back in a jiffy?" I mouthed to Mom.

Mom smiled. "Didn't you want a Coke or something?"

I shook my head.

"I'm sorry, honey," she said. "I wanted us to eat alone."

"Me too."

"I didn't know what to say to her. She's really nice. She means well."

"Let's not worry about it," I said.

Mom leaned forward. "It isn't a very good birthday treat, though. Let's go out to dinner tonight. Anywhere you want—just the two of us."

I smiled at her. "Okey-dokey," I said.

"Look at this!" Lou called from the bar. "They're giving me my very own tray!" She started over to us. "Next thing you know, people are going to start giving me their dinner orders." She took the drinks off the tray, then sat down and took a long sip of hers. "Oh, that's *goood*," she said. "Bob laughs at me for drinking piña coladas. He calls them sissy drinks. Mackie, don't ever order one when y'all go out. He'll embarrass you to death!"

"Who's Bob?" I said.

"Lou's brother," Mom said. "Did you and Sally get a game in this morning?"

"No, we couldn't get a damn court!"

"Why not?"

"Too many signed up. They've got to get better organized in that pro shop and not sign so many up. I was tempted to go ahead and sign up you and Bob to play with me and Chuck tomorrow."

"You play tennis with Bob?" I asked Mom.

"Not much—"

"You'd think they played all the time! Y'all are a good team! They slaughtered us last week, Blue," Lou said. "Oh—when is he coming back from New York tonight? Do you know what time?"

"Nine, I think," Mom said. I stared at her, but she didn't look at me. I felt my chest start to tighten.

"So y'all won't make it to Tina Redbeck's barbecue?" Lou said.

Mom shook her head.

"Does Bob live in New York?" I asked my mother. She shook her head again, still not looking at me.

"*Bob* live in New York?" Lou said. "Lord, no! He despises that city. He calls it the 'rotten apple'!"

I stared at Lou for a few seconds, then said, "My father lives in New York."

She smiled and took a sip of her drink.

"He lives in Greenwich Village. He really likes it," I said.

"That's nice," Lou said.

"He's lived there since February." I felt like I was backing Lou up against the wall. "He moved there because he hated this town."

"Blue!" Mom said.

"What?" I turned angrily. Who was this Bob to her?

"Just relax," she said, laughing uneasily. "Maybe we should all decide what we want for lunch." She opened her menu. Lou opened her menu too. I flipped mine open and glared at it.

"I guess I'll have the chicken salad," Mom said.

"Oh, that sounds good," Lou said. "What about you, Blue?"

"I'm not hungry now." I put my menu down and pushed my chair back from the table. "I have to go to the ladies' room."

"You do?" Mom said.

"Yes, excuse me." I stood up and hurried across the dining room floor. I crossed the lobby, then turned the corner and went through a door that said POWDER ROOM.

The "Powder Room" was all in pink—pink walls, pink lights, a pink Kleenex box on the glass-topped dresser. There was the sweet odor of rose-scented spray in the air. I sat at the dresser and dropped my head onto my bare arms.

A minute later the door opened. "What's wrong?" my mother said.

"I'm sick."

"Why are you sick?"

"I'm nauseated. I want to leave now."

"Oh no, honey, we can't leave now. We can't be rude to Lou."

"I don't care about her. She's a bitch."

"Blue, don't say that!"

"Well then, what's all that stuff about you and her brother?"

"He's just a friend of mine."

"It sounds like you're dating him."

"Please, Blue, don't start accusing me of things now. . . ."

"You are dating him, aren't you?"

"Blue, don't be this way. Please. You make my life terrible sometimes."

"You make my life terrible all the time!" I yelled. I stood up and nearly fell over. I felt dizzy.

"Shhh—" Mom said. "People will hear."

"I don't care what people hear. I hate this place!"

"Hush!"

"You're really sinking low joining this crappy place. No wonder Dad never wanted to come here!"

"Blue, stop it."

"I don't blame him. I'd go to New York too if I were him. Nothing could be worse than this. I should have gone with him!"

"You don't know what you're talking about."

"I do too. I hate it here. I wish I were with Dad!"

"Blue, you know he can't take care of you!"

"He can so!" I cried. I grabbed her arms. "You're the one who can't take care of me. *You!*"

"Let go of me," she said.

"You're the one!" I was crying.

"Let go, Blue!"

I heard the door open. "Mackie?" Lou said.

I whirled around and went into a toilet stall and closed the door.

"Is everything all right?" Lou said.

"Yes, we'll be out in just a minute, Lou," Mom said.

"Oh, good," Lou said. I heard her leave.

"Blue?" Mom stood on the other side of the stall door. "Are you coming out?"

I wiped my eyes with toilet paper. "There's something I didn't even tell you about Dad," I said.

"What?"

"He might get his play done. He told me not to tell you. He wanted to surprise you."

"What do you mean?"

"Someone's interested in his play. I talked to him on the phone this morning. There's a reading of his play tonight, and he wanted to surprise you!"

"Well—that's great," she said. "I'm glad to hear that."

I could tell she wasn't.

"Are you coming out of there?" she said. I blew my nose, then opened the stall door.

"Oh, honey—your hair's coming all undone," Mom said sadly. She went over to the dresser and took her brush out of her purse. "Here," she said.

I pulled out all my pins and brushed my hair.

"There—you look nice now," Mom said.

I didn't.

"Will you come back with me now and try to eat

some lunch?" she said. "I promise we'll leave as soon as we can."

"Okay."

"Thank you, honey." She held the door open for me. We walked across the lobby and through the Players' Lounge.

"Oh good—there y'all are!" Lou said. "I ordered your chicken salad, Mackie."

"Thank you," Mom said as we sat down.

"I took the liberty of ordering you one too, Blue."

"Thank you," I said, staring down at the table.

"I have a niece in Charleston, Blue, about your age. She's coming up in a few weeks."

I didn't say anything.

"Mackie, have you ever been to Charleston?" Lou said.

The two of them started talking about Charleston. I didn't say much during the meal. Lou took care of most of the talking. She yapped away between us like a terrier, yapped, ate, and yapped—till I wished I could take off my sneaker and just flatten her.

5

Mom put her coffee cup down and looked at her watch. "Well, I guess we'd better go," she said. "I promised Walter we'd stop by his office for a minute." I hoped she was just saying that for an excuse to get away from Lou. I wasn't about to go with her to Uncle Walter's.

"It must be nice having a lawyer for a brother," Lou said. "Let him handle all your affairs." She hooted and covered her mouth as if she'd just made a joke without meaning to. She was a moron. I stood up to leave.

"Wait a minute, Blue," Mom said. "I have to sign the check."

"Oh, Mackie, please—let me," Lou said. "It can be my birthday present to Blue." Lou winked at me.

"Oh, thanks, Lou. You're sweet." Mom looked at me, waiting for me to thank Lou.

"Thanks," I said.

"You're welcome, Blue. It was a real pleasure meeting you!"

I didn't say anything.

"Well, bye-bye, hon," Mom said, patting Lou on the shoulder.

"Say hi to Walter and Margaret for me."

"I will." Mom waved and left the table. I followed her without saying good-bye to Lou.

"We're not really going to Uncle Walter's office, are we?" I said as we walked to the car.

"Just for a minute," Mom said. "He wants to give you something for your birthday."

"Oh, Mom, I don't want to go there now!"

She stopped and faced me. "It's just for a minute. You can stand it for a minute."

"But he's the last person I want to see on my birthday."

"Oh, don't be so hateful," she said. "You don't like anybody. These people aren't your enemies."

"*He* is."

"Oh, he is not. Look, I promised him we'd stop by. If you can't tolerate seeing him, you can just wait in the car."

"I don't want to wait in the car."

"Then you can just walk home, dammit." She turned and walked away from me toward our car.

"All right, I will," I said, following her.

She opened the car door and looked for her keys in her purse. "Okay, you know how to get there from here?" she said.

"Yes. . . ." I dreaded the thought of walking home. I could just see myself—a giant stick figure loping around the golf course. "You really want me to walk home? On my birthday?" I said.

"Walk or come with me to Walter's for just two minutes."

I stared at her and didn't say anything.

"All right," she said. She got into the car. She slammed the door and put her keys into the ignition and started the motor. "See you back at the house," she said. She started backing out of her parking space.

"Mom—wait!" I said angrily.

"You want to come?"

"I'll wait in the car while you go in. But you better hurry." I went around and got in the front seat. I glared at the club as Mom pulled out of the parking lot. "I don't know why you're so eager to go to Walter's," I said.

She sighed.

"You going to sign some more separation papers or something?"

"Oh, please. Would you stop?" Mom said.

"No. You've told me to tell you what I'm thinking."

"Well, why are your thoughts always so angry?"

"I don't know. I just know I still love Dad, even if you don't."

"Oh, damn," Mom said softly. She pulled over to the side of the road and shut off the ignition.

"I know you love him," she said. "But there's nothing we can do about that right now."

"Yes, there is."

"What?"

"I can go visit him."

She put both her hands on the steering wheel,

stared straight ahead, and then looked back at me. "I don't think he really wants you up there now, honey."

"He does want me there. He told me this morning that if his play gets done, he wants me to come visit him."

"If his play gets done? Only if his play gets done?"

"What's wrong with that?" I yelled. "He just wants me to be proud of him!"

"Okay, okay. We'll see about all that when the time comes."

"*Mom*, he's my father! I have a right to see my own father, and he has a right to see me!"

"He gave up that right, Blue, when he abandoned you and me."

"Oh—so now Uncle Walter's making it so Dad can't legally see me, right?"

"Don't blame Uncle Walter for anything. He's just acting as my lawyer."

"But he loves it."

Mom groaned and banged her head against the steering wheel. "We've been through this," she said. "Dad didn't leave because of Walter. You're not facing reality."

I stared at the golf course and didn't say anything.

"Listen, Blue. Dad was having lots of problems before he left, serious problems. You know he was, Blue."

"He didn't have lots of problems."

"Blue, a person has problems when he can't sleep—when he goes for long periods of time not talking to his wife—when he walks all over the city in the middle of the night. Betty Morgan saw Dad wandering the golf course at three o'clock one morning."

"What was she doing out there?"

"That's not the point. She was driving home from a party."

"He was just lonely," I said. "He didn't fit into this snobby life here—it was crushing him."

"He was crushing himself, honey."

"No, he wasn't. You should never have made him move here!"

"Oh, I hate this," Mom said, hiding her face against the steering wheel. "I hate it." She knocked her forehead against her hands a few times, then looked at me. "We're not getting anywhere. You want me to drive you home now? I'll be glad to."

I shook my head.

"Well, what do you want to do?"

"I want to go to Uncle Walter's office."

"What do you mean—you want to go to Uncle Walter's office?"

"I want to ask him something. I want to ask him why he told Dad to leave us."

"What?" She looked at me as if I were crazy.

"Well, you tell me I'm not facing reality."

She stared at me for a few seconds. "Okay. It might do some good if we all had a talk. Walter's tried to talk to you about all this before, but you wouldn't listen to him."

"I'll listen to him now."

"Good. But please don't act ugly."

"Don't worry—I won't act ugly," I said.

6

"Hi, Lolly," Mom said to the receptionist as we stepped out of the elevator into Uncle Walter's plush office.

"Well, hey there!" Lolly said. "You just about missed us. We're getting ready to leave for the day." She picked up the phone. "Someone out here to see you, Mr. Larue. There's a strong family resemblance." She winked at me and Mom. "All right." She hung up. "He'll be right out," she said.

A moment later Uncle Walter came out to us. "Hi, ladies," he said. He looked scrubbed and shining in a pair of kelly-green golfing pants and a white shirt. "What have y'all been doing this pretty day?" His pink face beamed as he looked from me to Mom.

"Oh, we did a little shopping and went to the club for lunch," Mom said.

"Doesn't that sound good?" Walter said, beaming at me. His beaming had no connection to reality. There was nothing to beam about now. Walter was like one of the crickets I'd told Mom about last night. His voice seemed to come from his body, but I felt that if I really went looking for him, I wouldn't be able to find him.

"Why don't y'all come on back? Sugar, you can go on home," he said to Lolly.

"Thanks, boss. See you Monday. 'Bye, ladies. Have a good weekend."

"You too, Lolly," said Mom.

I trailed after Mom and Uncle Walter into his office. "Y'all have a seat," he said. He sat behind his huge desk and took out his checkbook and started writing in it. The office was lit by a green-shaded lamp, and the air was cool with air conditioning. The warm, sunny June day outside had been completely shut out.

Walter ripped the check from his checkbook and held it out to me. "Happy birthday, young lady."

I took it from him. I thought it would be rude to look at the amount, so I folded the check in half and said, "Thank you."

"Aren't you even going to look at it?" Mom said.

"Well, okay." My face felt hot as I unfolded the check. "It's for fifty dollars," I said, embarrassed. Mom and Walter laughed.

"I hope you have a real nice birthday, sugar," he said.

"Thank you."

"Walter," Mom said, "before we go, there are some things Blue would like to discuss with you."

"Mom . . ." I could have killed her. I didn't feel like talking about Dad now—especially after that stupid business with the check.

"Oh?" Walter said. "What is it, sugar?"

"I—I guess I don't feel like talking about it anymore," I said.

"Honey, you're not on the witness stand," Mom said. "Just talk to Uncle Walter like he's family. We're all a family."

"No, we're not," I said. "You and Dad are my family."

Walter leaned back in his chair and started playing with a pencil.

"Oh, honey . . ." Mom said.

I looked at her for a few seconds, then I looked at Uncle Walter. "I just wanted to ask you something," I said to him. "I wondered why you told my dad he should leave us."

"Sugar, I didn't tell Richard to leave y'all," he said quietly.

"Well, you told him that he was making us unhappy. But he wasn't making me unhappy. I was happy when he was living here. I got unhappy when he left. So you're the one who's made me unhappy, not him."

Mom laughed nervously. "Want to run that by us once more?" she said.

I hated her for making fun of me now. "I said— Uncle Walter is the one who's made me unhappy, not Dad." I spoke sharply so she wouldn't make any more jokes. "We used to be a pretty close family before we moved here," I said to Uncle Walter. "In Chapel Hill we went to movies together and bookstores a lot, and Dad worked on his plays, and Mom was even in some plays at the community theater—"

"Blue," Mom interrupted me. "Let's not talk about all that."

"But I have all these good memories of us. Remember when Dad bought the red Chevette and you guys picked me up after school and we rode around in it? Remember it was cold and gray, and when we got home, we made a fire and looked at the owner's manual together?"

"I don't see the point of going into all this now," Mom said.

"I just want to prove to Uncle Walter that we were a pretty happy family—you and me and Dad. You said we should have a talk."

Walter leaned forward in his chair. "Sugar, believe me, I never wanted to break up your family."

"But you did," I said. "You had a big fight with Dad—you told him he was making us unhappy, and he left the very next night."

Walter stared at me, frowning. "Blue, your daddy had some real problems for quite some time—"

"But everybody has problems. You have problems. Mom has problems. I have problems. You guys just keep saying Dad has problems so you won't feel guilty for making him leave. I can understand why you would say that," I said to Walter. "But I can't understand why Mom says it." I looked at her. "You loved him once, didn't you? You loved his familiar face—"

"Blue, let's end this."

"Didn't you love his habits—like his toothbrush always being chewed up, even just a couple of days after he'd bought a new one? I don't understand why it doesn't drive you crazy remembering little things like that. I can hardly stand it. What about you, Mom?"

She looked embarrassed.

"You don't feel terrible when you remember that stuff?"

"Oh, Blue," she said.

"But you'd rather be with people like Lou, wouldn't you?"

"Blue, stop."

"I feel like you traded our family for this town. You gave up all our memories and all our love for this—this junk."

Mom stood up and walked out of the room. She was crying as she left. Walter stared at me. "Blue, that's real unfair of you and you know it."

I stared back at him. He was so dumb, I thought.

"Well, I better go check on Mackie." He stood up and left the office.

I stared out the window at the pine trees and sunlight. I felt hardhearted and free of guilt—as if I had just hurt my mother for her own good.

"Blue?" Mom said after a minute.

"What?" I turned. Mom and Walter were standing in the doorway of his office.

"Let's go now," she said.

I got up and went to her. Uncle Walter looked miserable. For once he'd stopped beaming. "Thank you for my birthday present," I said to him.

He nodded.

Mom turned and started down the hall ahead of me.

" 'Bye," I said to Uncle Walter, and I took off after her.

7

We drove home in silence. Mom wiped her eyes a couple of times, but I pretended not to notice. When the car came to a stop in front of the porch, I grabbed my shopping bags out of the backseat and got out. I waited for Mom to lead the way into the house.

She went straight back to the kitchen. I went up to my room and threw my stuff on my bed. Then I decided to go back downstairs and try to make up with Mom.

I stood in the doorway and watched her crack a tray of ice cubes down on the Formica counter. She glanced up and saw me, but then she looked down again and lifted a couple of cubes from the tray, careful not to touch them with her coral-colored nails. She dropped them into a glass, then poured herself a drink. She walked to the back door and looked out at her flower garden.

I sat at the kitchen table and started drumming my fingers against one of the plastic mats. "Well," I said after a while. "What do you want to do now?"

Mom shrugged her shoulders and took a sip of her drink.

"I guess we shouldn't fight on my birthday," I said softly.

I thought I heard her say, "Hmm."

"What?" I said.

"Nothing," she said.

"You still want to go out to dinner with me?" I said.

She didn't answer.

"You said we could go for a birthday treat since Lou ate lunch with us."

She turned and looked at me without smiling. "Where do you want to go?" she said.

"Well—I was thinking maybe we could get a little pizza."

"Can we have a pleasant meal?"

"Yes."

"All right then," she said faintly.

"Maybe we could go to a movie too," I said.

She nodded.

"I'll get the paper and see what's on." I jumped up and hurried to the porch and grabbed the afternoon paper.

"Let's see," I said, coming back into the kitchen. I wrestled the paper open to the movie page. "Oh! How about that new Paul Newman movie?"

"That's okay with me. What time does it start?"

"Let's see—there's a seven-o'clock show. That's good, isn't it? It gives us time to go and have a leisurely meal first at Pizza Hut."

She almost smiled. "A leisurely meal at Pizza Hut?"

"Yes."

"I want to change first," she said.

"Good idea. Slip into something a little more comfortable."

This time she did smile—grudgingly. Then she put her glass down and left the room.

At Pizza Hut we shared a large pepperoni pizza. We commented that the air conditioning was too cold, and we laughed at a baby in a high chair at the next table. When we'd finished our pizza, I asked Mom what time it was.

"Six fifteen," she said.

"Oh—then we'd better go, so we can get good seats. Remember, it's Saturday," I said.

We dumped our paper plates and cups into the garbage bin, then headed out to the parking lot. "Thanks for my birthday dinner," I said. Mom nodded and put her hand against my back as we walked to the car.

We drove to the mall and parked in front of the Twin movie theaters. "See—there's already a line," I said.

We got out of the car and headed to the back of the line of people waiting to buy tickets. We were almost to the end when I stopped: Susan and that guy Tony from Hardee's were standing in line talking. Behind them was Mike, the John Travolta guy. He had his arm around a big-breasted blond girl.

I whirled around and took off in the opposite direction. "Mom—come!" I said.

"What's wrong?"

"Come!" I hurried away from the theater. I heard Mom's wooden sandals clacking after me, but I didn't dare look back at her. I walked to the other side of a pickup truck where no one could see me.

"What's happening?" Mom said when she joined me.

"Susan was at the end of the line with those two guys from Hardee's last night and another girl!"

"Is that terrible?"

"Yes! What do you think?"

"But I thought you didn't like those guys."

"I don't, but it doesn't matter! I don't want them to see me!"

"Well, I think you look real pretty tonight," she said.

"That's not it—it's that it's Saturday night, and I don't have a date. I'm here—" I stopped.

"Ohhh." Mom smiled. "With your mother." She reached out and gave me a little hug. "Well, to hell with them. We'll just go home and make popcorn and watch Home Box. What do you say?"

"That would be great."

"Let's go."

"Wait, Mom. I don't want them to see me walking to the car. Can we wait here until the line goes inside?"

"Why don't you stay here, and I'll get the car and bring it around?"

"Oh, that's a good idea," I said.

"I'll be right back." She took off between two rows of cars. I had to laugh as I watched her—she was keeping her head down and was walking real fast as if she were afraid of being seen too.

When Mom and I got home, we made popcorn and watched an old movie, *Tammy and the Doctor*. We had a good time together making fun of it. We didn't talk about my dad at all. I kept thinking about him, though, wondering how his play reading was going.

When I went up to bed around midnight, I decided to sneak a call to him. I dialed his number, but there was no answer. Before going to sleep, I imagined myself wearing a long dress to a smoky, dimly lit New York restaurant. Everyone was talking and having a good time. Someone toasted my dad's play—glasses clinked—and I pictured my dad laughing.

8

Sunday morning while Mom was at church, I tried calling Dad every fifteen minutes, but there was never any answer. Between my attempts to reach him, I sat on the porch and studied for my English exam, rereading parts of *My Ántonia*. I'd loved that book when I'd read it last month, but this morning I didn't care about it. The only important thing to me was finding out what had happened with Dad's play. I put the book down for the tenth time and went into the house to try his number again. But just as I picked up the receiver in the hall, I heard Mom pull into the driveway.

I hung up and went back out to the porch and sat down. "What are you doing?" Mom said as she climbed the steps.

"Studying for my English exam."

"Good for you. Want some lunch?"

"No, thanks. Maybe later."

"Well, I'll leave something out for you. I'm going to have a quick bite, then I'm going out for a little while."

"Where are you going?"

"Over to Walter and Margaret's." She looked at me a little defensively.

"Oh," I said simply, and I went back to my book. I was glad to hear she was going out. I wanted to be by myself when I talked to Dad.

After Mom went inside, I closed my book. I walked back to the TV room and lay down on the couch and waited for her to leave for my aunt and uncle's. "I'm leaving now!" she called after a few minutes.

"Come here—let me see you."

She poked her head into the TV room. "Are you taking a little break?"

"I'm finished. Let me see how you look."

Mom stepped all the way into the room and turned around. She was wearing a wine-colored sundress—it looked good with her tan. "Do I pass inspection?" she said.

"Not bad. You could do worse."

"Gee, thanks." She laughed. "I'll remember that when I start feeling insecure." She started to leave.

"What's going on over there? A party?" I called after her.

"Not really. I'll see you later, honey. 'Bye!"

I jumped up and peered through the venetian blinds until her car had pulled out of the driveway. Then I hurried to the hall phone and dialed Dad's number. It rang and rang. I was just about to hang up when he answered. He sounded out of breath.

"Dad?" I said.

"Blue?"

"Hi. I've been trying to call you."

"You have? Let me catch my breath. I just got in."

"I was just wondering how everything went last night."

"Last night? Oh, you mean the reading?" he said.

"Yes. Did it go well?"

"Yeah. Darn—I was supposed to call you, wasn't I?"

"That's okay. Everyone liked the play?"

"Yeah, I think so. Not too many complaints."

"Well, do you think the director will do it off-off-Broadway?"

"He seems pretty interested, birdie. I'm going to have breakfast with him this week so we can talk about the whole thing."

"Oh, that's great, Dad! It sounds like things are starting to happen, doesn't it?"

He laughed.

"It does!" I said. "I think it does."

"Oh, you do, huh?" His voice got soft. "Well, you're a bluebird, you know that?"

"Yeah," I said. I wondered if he was going to say anything about me going up there when they did his play.

"Did you have a nice birthday?" he said.

"It was pretty good. I had a long talk with Mom about some things."

"What things?"

"Oh, about you and stuff." I didn't want to tell him we'd had a big fight about my seeing him.

"What about me?"

"You know, about some of my memories about you and stuff like that."

"Like what memories?"

"Oh, just little things—like about your toothbrush—how it's always chewed up . . ."

"Rich memories," he said, laughing.

I giggled. "Don't laugh," I said.

"So what did Mackie say when you shared these memories with her?"

"She cried."

"She did?"

"Yeah."

"Hmm. Must have been because they were so paltry."

"Oh, Dad—" I laughed again.

"Hey—I wish I could see you right now," he said.

"You do?"

"Yes. Right this minute, eat you up with my eyes and see you laugh."

"Well, when they do your play, you'll want me to come up there, right?"

"Absolutely."

"Okay, I will," I said.

"You think Mom will let you?" he said.

"Yes, I think she will. Will you call me and tell me how your meeting goes with the director?"

"Sure."

"Promise?"

"I promise, babe. I'm sorry I didn't call you first thing today. I love you," he said. I knew this was a signal he was about to hang up.

"I love you, too. I'm studying for my exams now,"
I said, to keep us going a little longer.

"Oh yeah? Good. Well . . . I'll talk to you later."

"Okay. You'll call me?"

"Sure, babe. I'll call you," he said.

" 'Bye, Dad."

" 'Bye, bluebird," he said, and he hung up.

I went out to the porch and leaned against one of
the white columns, closing my eyes to the sunlight.
I was so relieved Dad's reading had been a success.
I wanted to share the news with Mom—convince her
that he was a different person in New York. He'd
actually sounded happy on the phone.

I thought maybe I'd go over to Uncle Walter's so I
could tell Mom. I wanted Uncle Walter and Aunt
Margaret to hear about the play too. I hurried up to
my room to change my clothes. As I dressed, I pictured Dad's play reading—I wished I'd been there.
Dad's New York friends would probably like me, I
thought. Going up there could be the beginning of
a different life for me. I pictured myself someday on
a talk show, laughing about how I'd been ignored in
Layette: "Johnny, I just couldn't get into flipping
french fries in the backseats of VW's." Or I'd be
written up in a *TV Guide* interview: "Well, it wasn't
until I went to New York that I really blossomed. I
remember it was June and I was fifteen, tall and sort
of gangly. . . ."

9

I hurried toward Uncle Walter and Aunt Margaret's, around the golf course in the shadows of the pine trees bordering the fairway. When I came within sight of their white brick house, I was surprised to see lots of cars in their driveway. Mom had said they weren't having a party—she must have meant they weren't having a big party. I hadn't actually been invited to the party, but I told myself that if they really considered me "family," I didn't have to be invited. Mom might even be pleased that I was making an attempt to be sociable.

When I got to the back door, I could hear laughter and chatter coming from inside the house. I knocked on the kitchen door and Tippy, Margaret's terrier, started barking at me from his pen. "Hey there, Tippy. What are you barking at me for?" I said in a high baby voice, trying to sound as if I knew my way around here.

I poked my head inside the kitchen. Nancy Jennings, Margaret's maid, was doing the dishes. She hadn't heard me knock. "Hi, Nancy," I said.

"Oh, hi, Blue! How are you doing?"

"I'm doing fine. How are you getting along?" I said, stepping inside.

"Fine, just fine." She put a clay casserole dish on the counter to dry. Margaret's kitchen had dark wood cabinets and copper pots hanging from overhead. I would have liked it if it had been someone else's kitchen. But in my aunt's house even the neat stuff seemed fakey.

"I didn't expect to find so many people over here," I said to Nancy.

"Good gracious—it's Blue!" Aunt Margaret came bustling into the kitchen with a tray of half-empty dip bowls. "What in the world do we owe this honor to?"

"I just thought I'd drop in and say hi."

"Does your mother know you're here?"

"No, ma'am, I just decided to come by on the spur of the moment."

"Oh . . . Well, wait right here and I'll run get her—"

Before I could say anything, Aunt Margaret hurried out of the kitchen.

"So what are you doing with yourself these days, Blue?" Nancy said. "I've missed seeing you."

"I know," I said. "I haven't come around much lately."

"How's school?"

"Fine, it's out this week. My last exam is on—"

"Honey," Mom interrupted me as she came into the kitchen. "What's wrong?"

"Nothing's wrong. I just wanted to come by."

She stared at me.

"What is it?" I said.

"Blue—are you spying on me?"

I felt as if she'd just slapped me. I backed a step toward the doorway. "No, I'm not spying on you."

"Then why did you come by here?"

"I wanted to tell you that—that I just talked to Dad and he's happy because his play went real well last night."

"Oh, it did?" She looked confused. "I'm sorry—"

"I wasn't spying on you!"

"Mackie?" A large man entered the kitchen. He was sunburned and wore a Lacoste shirt and neatly pressed slacks. His blond hair was perfectly cut. "There you are, darlin'," he said, walking over to Mom. He noticed me standing in the doorway. "Oh, hi," he said.

Mom sighed. "Bob," she said, "this is Blue."

"Oh. Hi, Blue." The man stuck out his large hand for me to shake. I gave him mine. He squeezed it firmly, then let it go.

Aunt Margaret came into the kitchen. "Oh, Bob— I was looking for you!" she said nervously. "You want to join me out here a minute, honey? I have something to show you."

"Sure, Mag," he said. "Nice meeting you, Blue. 'Scuse me." He touched Mom's elbow, then followed Margaret out of the kitchen.

I stared at Mom. I could hear Bob and Margaret's conversation trail off into the noise of the party.

"Well?" Mom said. "That was Bob."

"You said yesterday he was just your friend."

"He is my friend."

"He called you darlin'."

"Blue . . ."

"You like him a lot?" I said.

"Yes. I like him. He's really nice, Blue."

"You like him more than Dad?"

"Honey, can we talk about this later?"

"Do you?" I said loudly.

Mom whirled away from me, pushed open the back door, and stepped outside. Tippy started barking at her from his pen. I followed her out onto the back stoop. "Do you?" I said.

"Look, when I get home, we'll talk, okay? We'll really discuss all this." She looked at me pleadingly.

"Just tell me—" I said. "Tell me the truth."

She sighed. "What do you want me to tell you, Blue?"

"Tell me once and for all that you don't love Dad anymore and we'll never be a family again. Tell me, so I can give up hoping that we'll ever be together, all of us. Just tell me."

"All right. I don't love Dad anymore. I will never live with him again, Blue. I'm sure of it. I want to live a different life than he does. So please stop hoping that we'll get back together."

I didn't say anything.

I started down the steps.

"Where are you going?" she said.

I didn't answer her. Tippy went wild barking as I ran down the driveway.

10

When I got home, I went straight to my room and fell facedown on my bed. I couldn't stand the thought of my mother with that clone, Bob—his football player's body, his perfect hair, his expensive clothes. How could she prefer a phony guy like that to my dad? My dad was a real person even when he was unhappy. He was sensitive and honest and artistic. He was worth a million Bobs.

Breathing hard, I sat up and reached for my phone. I put it on my pillow and dialed my dad's number. When he answered, I said, "Dad?"

"Blue?"

"How are you?" I said.

"Fine. What's wrong?"

"I was just wondering how you were."

"I just talked to you a little while ago. Is everything okay?"

"Dad—"

"What, Blue?"

I started crying.

"My God, what is it?" he said.

"Can I come up there—right away?"

"Why, Blue?"

"I want to be with you. Even if you and Mom aren't together, I don't want you and me not to be together."

"Did something happen down there?"

"No. I just want to see you. Now. I don't want to wait for your play anymore, Dad. Please let me come now."

"Sure, you can come. But what does Mackie say about all this?"

"She's not here. But it doesn't matter if she wants me to go or not. I don't care anymore what she wants."

"Okay, babe, calm down. Tell me what happened."

"Oh, we had a fight, but I feel like we fight all the time now. We don't agree on anything. Do you want to see me, Dad?"

"Yes. God, yes. I always want to see you. But I have to warn you—I live in a pretty crummy place, Blue. It's small and there's paint peeling everywhere. You'd hate it. You've never been in a place like this before," he said.

"I don't care what it looks like. I'll like it better than this. I hate this house. I never feel happy here!" I said.

"God, I would love to see you," he said softly.

"Well, when do you think I can come?"

"What about school?" he said.

"It's out next week."

"You want to come when it's out?" he said.

"Yes! I want to come as soon as possible."

"Blue, I can't imagine Mackie'll let you."

"She will."

"Well, okay, talk it over with her and see what she says, babe."

"Okay, then I'll call you back, Dad."

"Good."

After I hung up, I washed my face, then I went downstairs and sat in one of the porch rockers to wait for my mother to come home. In about thirty minutes she pulled into the driveway. I stared at her as she got out of her car and climbed the steps.

"Why did you come home?" I said. "Weren't you having a good time?"

"I came home because you spoiled the party for me."

"I'm sorry," I said coldly.

"Let me tell you something, Blue." She took a few steps toward me. "That man and I are little more than friends. He's a nice man—but even that shouldn't matter. I am trying very hard to start my life over again. And you are doing nothing to help me. Nothing."

I looked down at the floor.

"Instead, you watch me like a hawk and censor everything I do," she said. *"It's not fair."*

"Well, you're not being fair to me."

"Oh no? Oh no? I make room for your moods constantly. I take you shopping. I try to talk to you. I'm your servant practically, and you give me nothing but a hard time!"

"Well, you don't do the most important thing. You don't let me see Dad."

"I have reasons—good reasons—why I don't think you should be with him right now."

"Well, I think you're just jealous. I think you're afraid I'll want to stay and live with him instead of you."

She took a deep breath and her voice got soft. "Is that what you think? Is that what you really think?"

"Well, and you don't think he can take care of me. But I just called him, and he really wants me to come up there—even before he finds out about his play. As soon as possible."

She didn't say anything for a few seconds as she stared at me. Then she said, "Well, maybe you should go see him. Maybe I should let you."

"You don't mean that."

"I mean it, Blue. I really mean it. I should just let you go up to New York and figure some things out for yourself."

"Can I call him back and tell him I'm coming for sure?"

"Go ahead."

"Can I tell him I'm coming *now*—when school's out?"

"Go whenever you want," she said.

"For how long?"

"I don't care."

Her attitude made me nervous. "How about two weeks?" I said.

"Fine, fine. Go call him."

"Okay." I stood up. She stared at me as I walked past her into the house. I picked up the hall phone and dialed Dad's number.

"Hello?" he said.

"Dad, it's me again." I watched Mom as she came inside and headed up the stairs. "Mom said I could visit you."

"She did?"

"Yes."

"Why? I mean—why did she change her mind?"

"I don't know. . . . I guess she realizes I'm desperate."

"When are you coming?"

"As soon as school's out. It's over on Wednesday. Mom said I could stay for two weeks."

"Well . . . that's great. If you don't mind staying here. My place is really bad."

"I don't mind."

"Well, good. . . . I'd love to see you."

"I don't know about my flight or anything. Can I call you back and tell you?"

"Sure. Call me back."

"Well . . . I guess I'd better go." I listened for my mother upstairs; I wondered what she was doing.

"Okay. I can't wait to see you," Dad said.

"Me too. 'Bye, Dad."

" 'Bye, bird."

After we hung up, I walked slowly up the stairs. I could hear Mom moving around in her room. I went into my room and sat on my bed. I didn't like the way she had given in to me. It was almost scary.

"Mom, could you come here a minute please!" I called.

A moment later she stood in my doorway. "What?" she said.

"Don't you want to know about my conversation with Dad?"

"What about it?"

"He's happy I'm coming."

"Good."

"Well, what about my plane reservation and stuff?"

"What about it? Call Eastern Airlines and figure it out. Whatever you want is fine with me."

"*Mom*—"

"Blue, you make your own plans with your dad. I don't want anything to do with this."

"All right. I will," I said.

"Good." She turned and left me.

I lay back on my bed. My greatest desire was about to come true, and Mom was almost wrecking it by being so cold.

11

I planned for my trip by myself. I made my own plane reservations and then organized what I would take. I called my dad back and told him when I'd arrive. He sounded glad that I was coming, and he said he was shocked and pleased that Mom was really going to let me.

I tried to get Mom involved in my preparations, but she was still acting distant. At every opportunity I asked her for her opinion on something. She always answered me, but never with much feeling or enthusiasm. I tried not to be too bothered by her attitude.

Tuesday afternoon Susan and I went shopping for clothes to wear in New York. I'd asked Mom to go with us, but she had just given me her department store credit cards and told me to buy whatever I wanted. So after exams Susan and I caught a bus and rode downtown. I carried a fashion magazine with me and thumbed through it, looking for ideas on what to buy.

Susan jabbered away beside me. "When Wayne called me last night, I told him about Tony and me going to the movies—"

"Oh, you did?" I said. I stared at a picture of some models in flapper dresses and wide-brimmed hats.

"I said, 'Since you went to the beach and dated there, I don't see why I can't date other people too.' He said he didn't date at the beach, and I said, 'Liar, I know good and well you did.' "

Susan stopped and waited for a response from me, but I pretended to be absorbed in my magazine. I resented her talking so much about herself when I was in the middle of planning such an important trip.

"If he had just told me the truth about the beach, I wouldn't have tried to get back at him," Susan said.

I turned the page of my magazine and studied a picture of some models leaning against an old car dressed in bobby socks and circle skirts.

"Do you think I should have told him about Tony?" Susan said.

"I don't know." I closed my magazine. "I'm nervous," I said.

"Why?"

"About going to New York and seeing my dad."

"How's he feel about it?" she said.

"I don't know. He's glad, but I think he's embarrassed about his apartment."

"How come?"

"He said it was crummy. Paint's peeling off the walls."

"Yuk."

"I don't care," I said. "Things like that don't bother me."

"What will y'all do up there?"

"Go to plays probably, cafés, maybe Central Park." My voice trembled. I looked out the window. The idea of being in New York seemed overwhelming.

"What's wrong?" Susan said.

"I don't know. . . . I guess I'm a little scared."

"You shouldn't be scared," she said. "You'll have a fabulous time."

"What makes you think so?"

"Everyone'll love you up there. You'll fit right in."

"I hope so."

"What do you want to buy today?"

I opened my magazine. "I don't know," I said. "I don't have any clothes that look like these."

"Like what?"

"All these clothes—they look like costumes, like antique dresses. They're from the twenties and fifties. There's a long article here on wearing clothes that are 'out of context.' "

"What's that mean?"

"It means you take something out of one time in history and you wear it in another time. I think it's a big thing in New York."

"Sounds weird," Susan said.

"Well—what do you think I should wear?" I said.

"Calvin Klein jeans."

I made a face.

"You're right," she said. "But I wouldn't worry.

You're built like a model. You look good in anything."

"I wish I weren't so tall and skinny." I twisted my hair and lifted it to the top of my head. "You think I look like Audrey Hepburn this way?"

"Who's that?"

"An old movie star. Oh, here we are—"

Susan looked back at me as we headed up the aisle of the bus. "You do look sort of like a movie star," she said. "Maybe you'll be discovered by one of your dad's friends."

"Oh, sure." We giggled and stepped off the bus onto the sidewalk.

First we went to Belk's. But the dresses there were too cutesy, too preppy. "This is definitely not the image I want," I said as we flipped through the racks.

We found the same boring selections in the other store I had a credit card for.

"No, no, no," I said. "Dammit, I liked that idea of old clothes."

"Well, if you only have credit cards for two stores, I guess you'll just have to be satisfied with this stuff," Susan said.

"No, I hate all this stuff." I sighed and looked around the store. "Hey . . ." I said. "I've got an idea."

"What?"

"Aren't antique dresses mostly like old ladies' dresses? You know, silky and hanging loose with cloth belts and stuff?"

"Yeah, I guess," Susan said.

"Well . . ." I said, leaning toward her, "let's look in these stores—in the old ladies' sections!"

Susan covered her mouth and screamed. "Blue—you're crazy!" she said.

"Come on!" I pulled her through Thalhimer's to the Mature Women's department.

After we refused her help, a saleslady stood back and watched in confusion as Susan and I yanked dresses off the racks. We held them up and discussed them till finally we settled on two outfits. The first one was a white crepe dress with purple flowers. It looked a little like a bag on me, but we both thought it would be perfect with a purple cloth belt.

I also tried on a black silk skirt and a loose white blouse. "Wear that with fake pearls," Susan said.

"Of course," I said, looking in the mirror. I thought this outfit really resembled some I'd seen in the magazine.

"Oh, and here." Susan handed me a white straw hat with a wide brim to try on.

"That's perfect!" I said. "Can't you see me wearing this in the Sheep Meadow?" I giggled.

"What meadow?"

"Sheep Meadow. It's a big open field in Central Park where people fly kites and stuff. My dad wrote me about it."

"Oh, wow," Susan said. "Maybe you'll meet a cute guy who'll take you there."

"No, I don't think so," I said. "I'll just be happy to go there with my dad."

When we got home, we passed my mother in the upstairs hall. "Hi, Susan," she said.

"Oh, hi, Mrs. Murray," Susan said in the matronly voice she always used with grown-ups.

"What did you girls get?" Mom said.

"Well . . ." Susan's voice rose.

I sighed. "You probably won't like the stuff we got, but I love it."

"Let's see," Mom said.

Susan giggled nervously as the three of us headed into my room. I dropped the shopping bags on the bed.

"These things are really charming, Mrs. Murray," Susan said, hovering near my mother.

Mom sat on the edge of the bed and didn't say anything until both outfits were spread neatly across the bedspread. Then she shook her head and said, "Blue, these are old ladies' clothes."

"They're out of context, Mrs. Murray," Susan broke in.

"What, Susan?" Mom bit her lip.

"They're out of context. That means clothes that are taken from one time in history and used in another . . . I think." Susan looked at me. I nodded.

My mother started laughing. "Oh, Blue, this is so pathetic," she said, tears coming out of her eyes.

"Mom!" I said.

"Maybe I could find you a pair of Grandmother's support hose to wear with these," she said.

"Oh, Mrs. Murray!" Susan said, collapsing onto

the floor. She held her sides and giggled. I couldn't help it—I cracked up too. The three of us laughed for a long time. Sometimes the oddest things could make me feel close to my mother.

12

That night I panicked. I was lying in bed in the dark and suddenly I was afraid to go to New York, afraid of seeing my dad, afraid that I wouldn't know what to say to him or how to act, and that my mother was right—something was wrong with him. I grew so afraid, I couldn't sleep. I jumped out of bed and went into the hall.

My mother's light was on. I walked back to her room and stood in her doorway. She was lying in bed, reading. "What's wrong?" she said.

"Why did you say you'd let me go to New York and find things out for myself?" I said. "Do you want me to have a bad time?"

She put down her book and looked at me. "No, Blue. I don't want you to have a bad time."

"Then why did you say all those things?"

"I guess I was angry."

"I'm scared," I said.

"Come here."

I walked to her.

"Sit here," she said. I sat next to her on the bed. She tugged on the sleeve of my nightgown. "Why are you scared?" she said.

"I don't know how to act up there."

"Just be yourself."

"I don't know what myself is."

She smiled. "Just say and do what you feel like saying and doing."

"How do you think Dad will act?"

She sighed. "He loves you very much. I think he'll try to do the right things. You'll have to help him."

"You're not still angry with me?" I said.

She shook her head.

"Good." I stood up and started to leave her.

"Blue—"

"What?"

"You know you don't have to stay the whole time, if you don't want to. If you're not having a good time . . ."

"I know."

"Well, try not to worry," she said, "and get a good night's sleep. You'll need lots of energy for tomorrow."

"Okay. Good night, Mom."

"Good night, honey."

I went back to bed and listened to the crickets in the dark. I remembered the night my father had left us. He'd taken me to the old Carlisle Hotel for dinner. It was just the two of us. He'd worn his gray wool suit and I'd worn my red dress with the lace collar. He said I looked beautiful. Waiters in black jackets served us on silver trays. Neither of us said anything about him leaving that night—even though he'd packed his car that afternoon. At times during the meal I couldn't swallow, but I tried to pretend that everything was normal.

Only later did I show him my real feelings. I was crying alone in my room after we'd gotten back from dinner. Around eleven he came to me and said, " 'Bye, bluebird." I'd followed him out to the driveway and screamed at him not to go, but he'd left anyway.

Suddenly I couldn't wait to see him. I wasn't scared anymore. I was just anxious to hug him and be with him.

When I got home from my last exam on Wednesday, I charged up to my room and put on my jeans, my boots, and my new white silk blouse. I brushed my teeth, then wrapped my toothbrush in a Kleenex and packed it with my makeup. After a quick look around my room, I carried all my stuff down to the front hall and called out, "Mom, I'm ready!"

She came out of the kitchen, drying her hands. "Let me see how you look," she said.

"Don't laugh."

"I won't laugh. You look nice."

"You think this blouse is silly, don't you?"

"No, I don't."

"You like my jeans tucked inside my boots or out?"

"I like them out like you have them."

"You do?" I said.

"Yes!" she said.

"Well, I think we should leave now," I said.

"Honey, it's only three thirty. Your flight's not for another hour and a half."

"But if we wait till rush hour, we might get stuck in traffic!"

"Blue, you're still in Layette—we don't have a rush hour." Mom laughed. "This isn't New York."

"I know it isn't New York!"

"Well, we'll go now if it makes you feel calmer."

"I feel calm—I just want to get there on time. I'll put my stuff in the car."

"Wait a minute. I have to get something," Mom said.

"What?"

"Just wait right here." She started up the stairs.

"Well, hurry!" I said.

A minute later she came back down with a small gift-wrapped package. "What's that?" I said.

"A going-away present."

"A going-away present?"

She handed me the package. I unwrapped it carefully, opened the lid of a little box, and lifted out an old-fashioned black beaded purse.

"It was Grandmother's," Mom said. "I thought it might look nice with one of your new outfits."

I looked at her quickly to see if she was making fun of me, but she wasn't smiling. "It's one of my favorite things of hers," she said. "I wanted you to have it for New York—for when you go out with Dad at night."

"Oh," I said, staring at the purse. Tears blurred my eyes. "That's nice."

"Well, don't let it make you sad." She laughed a little.

I tried to laugh with her.

"I'll get my bag," she said softly, "and we'll go."

When we got to the airport, Mom let me out at the entrance so I could check in while she parked the car. She met me at the departure gate and we sat together in the black plastic chairs, waiting for my flight to be called.

"You have your traveler's checks in your purse?" Mom said.

"Yes."

"Remember to keep that little slip separate from them."

"Okay."

"And call me tonight."

"I will. I wonder if Dad looks the same," I said.

Mom smiled. "I don't imagine he's changed much in just four months."

"I don't remember very well how he looked when he left."

"Hmm."

"Do you remember how he looks?"

She nodded.

"Well, I guess I'll find out soon enough."

Neither of us said anything else until my flight was announced. Then I stood up and grabbed my bags with both hands. "Can you carry all that?" Mom said.

"Yeah, sure." The only problem was I couldn't hug

her. I wished I'd hugged her before I'd picked everything up.

"Well, 'bye, darling," Mom said, squeezing my arms and kissing my cheek. "Have a good time."

"Thank you for the purse."

"You're welcome. Have a good plane ride."

"Okay." I stumbled away, twisting my neck to look back at her. " 'Bye."

"Call me," Mom said.

"Okay." I almost bumped into someone. I smiled at Mom one last time, then walked out of the departure door.

On the plane I put my two bags in the overhead compartment and my purse under the seat in front of me. I sat next to the window and buckled my seat belt; then I tried to read the airline magazine.

When the plane lifted off the ground, I felt exhilarated. In just an hour and fifteen minutes we'd land in New York City. I pictured myself running into my dad's arms.

The stewardesses wheeled a drink cart down the aisle, and I ordered a ginger ale. I studied the motion sickness bag. The instructions on it were written in three different languages. If you were sick, were you really supposed to use the bag in front of everyone? I kept trying to read the flight magazine. I looked up from it now and then and thought about the clothes I'd brought. I fantasized about going to restaurants and Central Park with my dad. I was so excited, I couldn't really hold any thought for more than a second.

It didn't seem long before the pilot said, "We are now making our approach into the New York area." I couldn't see anything out the window but clouds.

"Please make sure that your seat backs and tray tables are in an upright position for landing," the stewardess said.

I closed my magazine, gripped one clammy hand with the other, and looked out the window. The plane tilted downward as we descended. We bumped through some clouds. It amazed me that the people around me seemed so calm. They were all reading or sleeping.

When we came out of the clouds, I saw the New York skyline. I thought I recognized the World Trade Center towers. Then we were over water. For a minute it looked like we were going to land in the water, but then we bounced roughly onto the end of a runway. The plane let out a loud roar, we coasted for a few minutes, and then it was over. Everyone started popping open their seat belts and standing up. My hands trembled as I looked at myself in my compact mirror. Then I got all my stuff together and bumped up the aisle after everyone else. "Thank you. Have a good day," the stewardess said as I walked off the plane.

I made my way awkwardly down a crowded, noisy corridor and into an area where people were greeting one another. I realized that Dad and I hadn't set up a specific place in the airport to meet. I stumbled over to a beige-tiled wall and stared at the commotion around me. I watched a family of Spanish-speaking people laughing and greeting each other and an elderly couple embracing. I watched a man and a woman hug a little boy in a cowboy hat.

Then I saw my dad. He was standing by the wall opposite me, peering down the corridor I'd just come from. He was wearing a pair of faded jeans and a plaid shirt I remembered—except it looked different in this setting.

"Dad!" I cried, and I rushed toward him like I'd been shot from a cannon. "Dad!" He turned and saw me and ran to me and grabbed me, and for a long time we held on to each other very tightly without talking.

13

"It's good to see you," Dad said, holding me out at arm's length. "You're taller."

"I'm a giant."

"No, you're not. You're beautiful," he said.

"You look nice too. . . . You look the same."

"Yeah?"

"You seem so familiar."

"Well, that's good—I guess."

"It is."

We just stood there for a moment, smiling at each other while everyone brushed past us. "Well, is this all your stuff?" Dad said. "Did you check anything?"

"No, this is everything."

He picked up both my bags and we walked together out of the airport. The weather felt like fall when we stepped outside. There was a pink, coppery light on everything and the air was nippy.

"We'll get a cab," Dad said, and he led me over to the curb, where there was a line of people waiting for taxis. As we waited, I gazed at my dad's profile. I loved the way his straight brown hair fell over his forehead and the way his eyes crinkled at the corners as he squinted in the sunlight. I thought he was handsome. He turned and caught me staring at him.

"This is a really big airport, isn't it?" I said.

"Yeah, it's pretty big."

It was our turn to get a cab. "The Village—Sheridan Square," Dad said as we climbed into the back-seat with our bags. "Take the Midtown tunnel."

The cab took off. I rested my arm on the bag between me and Dad and tried to think of what to say. Dad looked over at me and I smiled. "You look great," he said.

"You do too. . . . We said this already." I giggled.

"That's okay. You look better every time I look at you."

"Oh, sure."

Dad kept staring at me till I felt so shy, I had to look away.

The cab sped down the highway, bumping roughly over potholes and broken pavement. "This is a wild ride!" I said to Dad.

"It's New York," he said.

The cab careened around a curve. "Oh, wow," I said. In front of us was the skyline of the city.

"You like it?" Dad said.

"Yes!" I said, and before I could even think, I took his hand. Neither of us said anything or looked at each other as he laced his fingers through mine.

The rumble of cars echoed around us as we drove

through a big tunnel. When we came out, the cab bumped down crowded, noisy streets; the driver honked at pedestrians who jumped and hurried out of our way. We whizzed through a light that had already turned red, then swung around a corner. I sucked in my breath and squeezed the life out of Dad's hand.

"On the left, by the newsstand," Dad said to the driver; then he unlaced his fingers from mine and reached into his pocket for some money.

Pulling my bags along with me, I followed Dad out of the cab onto an island in the middle of the traffic. "Well, we could go straight to my place or we could get something to eat," he said. "What would you like to do?"

"It doesn't matter to me. Whatever you want."

"How about some pizza?"

"Okay."

"Come on." He picked up my bags and led us across the street. I stayed close to him as we passed a guy in rags asking people for money. Then we walked by a busy outdoor café, full of people eating and talking. Close to the café a vendor was selling old paperbacks from a blanket, and two girls were playing violins. One of their cases was open on the sidewalk with a sign in it that said SUPPORT THE ARTS. Dad stopped and dug into his pocket. He pulled out some change and dropped it into the open case.

"Thank you," one of the girls said as she played.

We passed a meat market, then a pet store with blue parrots and white cockatoos in the windows. "Oh, look," I said.

"Wild, huh?" Dad said, barely glancing at the birds. It amazed me. He seemed so accustomed to all this, he hardly bothered to look.

Dad stopped and pointed at a pizza restaurant with an old-fashioned neon sign in the window that said JOEY'S. "That's it," he said.

"Oh, it looks great," I said.

He led me across the street and into the restaurant. A fifties-looking jukebox was playing a Frank Sinatra song; and in the back a white-aproned cook rotated a big piece of dough in the air with his fists.

I followed Dad to an empty booth near the window.

"You know, you're really in for a treat," Dad said as I unfolded my menu. "This place has the best pizza in all of New York."

I laughed.

"I'm serious," he said.

"Really? What kind do you want to get?"

"Get whatever you want."

"How about pepperoni?" I said.

"Fine with me." Dad ordered our pizza, and a Coke for me and a beer for him; then he lit a cigarette.

I looked around the restaurant. On the wall next to us was a picture of Jack Nicholson and the pizza cook with their arms around each other. Next to them was a picture of Woody Allen and the same cook holding up a piece of dough.

"Woody Allen," I said.

"Yeah. This joint's crawling with stars."

I giggled.

The waiter brought us our drinks. After he left, I said, "Do you live near here?"

"Yeah. A few blocks away."

"Oh, so we can walk there. That's good. Do you park your car near your apartment?"

"No, I sold the car when I moved here."

"You did?"

"Yeah."

I looked away from him and stared at the neon sign in the window. There was no chance now he would ever drive that car home. There was no chance I'd ever see it in the driveway again.

"Blue?" Dad said.

"What?"

"What's wrong? What just happened?"

"Nothing."

"Something happened."

I looked back at him. "It's just that I had good memories about that car."

"Oh . . . I'm sorry, babe, but it costs too much to keep a car in the city. I'd have to pay almost half of what I pay in rent to keep it in a garage, and I never even need it really."

"I know. It's okay. It's dumb."

"It's not dumb," he said.

"I'll live," I said.

"Watch out. Hot!" The waiter slid our pizza tray onto the table and gave us little plates.

"It looks good," I said after the waiter left.

"Yeah, it does," Dad said.

I stared at the pizza, wondering how to pick up one of the gooey pieces and eat it gracefully.

"Take a slice," Dad said. "Here—use your silverware."

"Oh, good idea," I said. I scooped up a slice with my fork and knife and slid it onto my plate. "Aren't you going to have some?" I said.

"Maybe in a minute. I'm not that hungry."

"Oh." I cut a little piece of pizza and blew on it before I put it in my mouth. It was good, but I was too nervous to really enjoy it. Dad watched me as I kept eating. I wiped my mouth a neurotic number of times.

"How's your play?" I said finally.

"What do you mean?"

"Well, have you talked to the director any more?"

"No. I have to see him tomorrow. He wants me to make some changes."

"What kind of changes?" I said.

"I guess I won't know till I talk to him."

"How did you meet him?" I said. I was racking my brains to keep the conversation going.

"In a bar I used to hang out at."

"Did he hang out at the bar too?"

"Not really. He was a friend of the cook's."

"The cook?"

"Yeah, she's really an actress."

"Oh. What's her name?"

"Annie Lawrence."

"Oh," I said. "I don't think I've heard of her."

Dad laughed out loud. "Nobody has," he said. "Maybe you'll meet her. She's a neat lady."

"She is?"

"Yeah . . . We were seeing each other for a little while," he said.

"You were?"

"Yeah, but not anymore."

"Was she your girl friend?"

"Well—not really. I guess you could say we just enjoyed each other's company for a while. But then she kind of called it off."

"Oh." I took a long sip of my Coke. I shook the ice and sipped again.

"Does that bother you?" Dad said.

"No. It's just that I guess I never imagined you with a woman besides Mom."

"You know I still love Mom a lot, don't you?"

I nodded. I didn't want to talk about this. I was afraid he might ask me next if she was going out with anyone. "Do you like living in New York?" I said.

He looked at me for a second, then took out a cigarette. "Yeah, but it's tough. It can get really bleak sometimes."

"How come?"

"Well, for one thing, driving a cab's not the prettiest way to see the city."

"You drive a cab? I thought you worked in a bookstore."

"I know. That's what I told Mackie—cab driving would disgust her."

"Oh . . . well, I think it's neat. How come you decided to drive a cab?"

"Well, it's the easiest way to make some money

and still have some freedom. I'm taking a break from it now. If this play thing gets going, I could get an option of maybe a couple of thousand bucks. That would hold me for a while."

"That sounds great. I hope it happens."

"Me too, bluebird," he said. "Well, have you had enough?"

"Yes," I said. Half of our pizza was still left on the tray, but neither of us seemed to want it.

"Okay," Dad said, picking up the check. "Ready to see some squalor?"

"What?"

"My place."

I giggled. "Sure. I've been waiting four months to see your squalor."

Dad laughed and stood up. "Come on," he said. He left a ten-dollar bill with the check, then he grabbed both my bags.

"I'll take one," I said when we were out on the sidewalk. I took one of the bags from him, then grabbed his free hand. He squeezed my hand tightly as we headed across the street.

14

The sky was dark gray as my dad and I walked to his apartment. In the distance the Empire State Building was lit up with blue and red lights. None of the buildings in this neighborhood were very tall. They were all close together, and most of them had stoops.

Dad stopped in front of a light-yellow stucco building and said, "This is it." He led me up the concrete steps and unlocked the front door. I followed him into a narrow hallway and up a couple of flights of dimly lit stairs. He stopped outside a door on the third floor and put his key in the lock. "Don't be shocked," he said.

"Quit worrying—I won't be," I said.

He pushed open the door, then stepped inside and flicked on the overhead light. "God," he said, shaking his head.

We were standing in a kitchenette with a stove, a laundry-type sink, and a round table covered with a dingy plastic cloth. On the other side of the room was a double bed with an old blue bedspread. Next to the bed was a window and a metal desk with stacks of books on it. Paint was peeling off the ceiling in little curls.

"It's terrible, isn't it?" Dad said.

"Yes," I said.

He burst out laughing. "Thanks for your honesty."

"It's terrible, but I like it," I said. "It's like a monk's house."

"Yeah, that's me. A damn monk."

"It's like a place in a movie."

"Well, whatever it takes to make you like it," he said. "Wait till you see your room." He stepped into a little hallway and stood at the entrance of another room. "I usually use this for my so-called office." He went into the room and flicked on a lamp. The room was very tiny with just a bed and a bedside table.

"Great, huh?" he said.

I walked to the bed. He'd spread a faded Indian cloth over a little fold-up cot. At one end was a pillowcase stuffed with towels. When I picked it up, one of the towels fell out.

"Whoops," I said, stuffing the towel back into the case.

"Forget it," Dad said. "You can have my pillow. I'll take that thing."

"No, that's okay," I said. "This is good."

"I bet you feel like running out of here and going straight back to Mom."

"No!" I said. "I love this room. It's cozy."

"You love it, huh? Better not say that—or I'll keep you forever."

"Great," I said.

We caught each other's eyes for a second, then Dad looked away and clapped his hands together. "Okay, coffee? Do you drink coffee?"

"Sure." I didn't like coffee, but I didn't want to turn down anything he offered.

I followed him back into the other room. He put a kettle of water on the stove and turned on the fire. Then he grabbed two cups off hooks over the sink and spooned instant coffee into them.

I sat at the little kitchen table and looked at his long, narrow back. I loved watching him make our coffee. It was like he was back home in Layette, doing a normal little chore.

"Okay!" he said, turning to me. "That'll boil in a minute." He crossed his arms and leaned against the sink.

"Is there a park near here?" I said.

"Yeah—there's Washington Square," he said.

"Remember last summer when we used to take books to the park in Layette and read together?"

He nodded, smiling.

"I remember you were reading *The Brothers Karamazov*," I said.

"And what were you reading?"

"Probably some teenage romance." I laughed. "But I read better stuff now. I really liked that book you sent me—*Letters to a Young Poet*."

"I know. You told me in one of your letters. Remember you sent me some quotes from it? I loved your letters, by the way. I read some of them to my friends."

"You did?"

"Yeah." The kettle started whistling. Dad took it off the burner and poured water into our cups.

"Who'd you read them to?" I said, laughing a little.

"Oh, some people from the bar—" The phone rang, interrupting him. "Can you get that?" he said.

I went to the phone beside his bed and picked up the receiver. "Hello," I said.

"Blue? It's Mom."

"Oh, hi, Mom." I watched Dad put our cups on the table. "I was going to call you," I said.

"I know, honey. I just got a little impatient to talk to you. How was your trip?"

"It was great."

"Good, and how's everything in New York?"

"Great."

"Well, what have you two been doing?"

"Well, Dad met me at the airport and we took a cab into the city. Then we had dinner at a pizza restaurant that has the best pizza in New York." I glanced at my dad. He was sitting at the table now, watching me.

"That sounds nice. How's Richard doing?"

"Fine. His apartment's real nice."

Dad rolled his eyes and I giggled.

"How's he acting?" Mom said.

"What?"

"You know, how's he acting?"

"Fine!" I said impatiently. She made him sound like a criminal. "He's taking very good care of me."

"Is he still working at the bookstore?"

"Um . . . no . . . not anymore. He's going to get some money for his play."

"Oh, is that definite?"

"Yeah. Almost. You want to talk to him? He's right here." I wanted to get off the phone.

"No, that's okay. I'll let you go now. Maybe I'll call you tomorrow."

"Oh. Okay. I'll talk to you tomorrow, Mom."

" 'Bye, honey."

" 'Bye." I hung up and looked at my dad. "She says hi," I said.

"She didn't want to talk to me?"

"Yeah, she did. But she said she didn't want to keep us any longer."

"Is she going to call you every day to check up on you?" he asked.

"I don't know." I got up and moved back to the table and sat. I took a sip of coffee. Dad lit a cigarette. A siren screamed from the street and another sounded in the distance. "A lot of sirens," I said.

Dad nodded. "How did you convince Mom to let you come up here?" he said.

"She decided it wasn't fair to keep us from being together."

"Did you tell her about the play?"

"Yes."

"And what did she say?" He took a sip of his coffee.

"She thought it was great."

"She did?"

"Sure," I said.

"Does she ever say anything about coming up here?"

"Yeah, but she's pretty busy now."

"Doing what?"

"I don't know," I said a little grouchily. I wanted this conversation to end. "Taking care of the house and taking tennis lessons and stuff like that."

After a moment of silence Dad got up from the table and rinsed out his cup at the sink. He put the cup back on the hook, then just stared at the wall for a minute.

"Well, I guess I'll take a shower," I said.

"The bathroom's in through there," he said. "It's pretty small."

"That's okay. Do you have any more towels?"

"What?"

"I—I forgot to bring towels."

"Well, of course, Blue—I have towels." He walked to his bureau and yanked open a drawer. "Right here—plenty of towels," he said defensively.

"Oh. Great. Well, I only need one," I said.

His face broke into a little smile. "Just one?"

"Yes."

"Okay." He took out a towel and handed it to me. "Here," he said.

"Thanks. It's a nice towel," I said. "It's beautiful."

"Oh you—" Dad hooked his arm around my neck and hugged me to him. "I'm going to kill you," he said.

"Help," I said.

He kissed the top of my head, then moved away from me toward the bathroom. "Well, let's see what the hot water situation is in here," he said.

After my shower, I put on my robe and looked in on my dad. He was lying on his bed looking at the paper. "You going to bed now?" he said.

"I guess."

"What do you want to do tomorrow?"

"Anything's okay with me."

"I have to go to breakfast with the director in the morning, but when I get back, we'll do something, okay?"

"Okay. Could we go to Central Park?" I said.

"Sure, if you want to."

"Maybe the Sheep Meadow," I said.

"Okay."

"Well, good night," I said.

"Hey—" he said as I turned to go. "You saved my life coming up here—you know that?"

"How did I do that?"

"Because you're making me very happy."

"You're making me happy too," I said.

"Hmm. Well, good night, bluebird."

"Good night, Dad."

15

"Blue—"

I opened my eyes. My room was dark.

"Blue—I have to go now."

"Where?" I said.

"To my meeting."

"What time is it? Is it night?"

"No, babe. It's morning. It's almost ten."

"Oh," I said, sitting up. "Can you turn on my light?"

Dad flicked on the overhead light. He stood in my doorway dressed in his blue suit. "When will you be back?" I said, squinting at him.

"In a couple of hours. Will you be okay alone?"

"Sure."

"If you want to go out, there's a set of keys on the table."

"Go out by myself?"

"Yeah, if you want to—or you can wait till I get back."

"Okay. You look nice in your blue suit."

"Yeah?" He seemed nervous.

I thought his suit looked a little big on him. He must have lost weight since he'd left Layette. "I think you look great," I said.

"Well, I don't know about that. Look, I'll try to get home as soon as I can."

"Okay, don't worry about me."

"Thanks, babe. 'Bye."

" 'Bye. Good luck!"

I listened as he let himself out of the apartment, then I looked around at my room. It was depressing in the glare of the overhead light—cracked walls, no windows.

I got out of bed and went into my dad's room. I pressed my cheek against the dusty window screen and looked outside. I watched my dad come out of the building, cross the street, and go around the corner. It looked so alive at the end of the street, full of cars and people—this was New York. I decided I'd go out for a walk.

When I stepped out the front door of the apartment building, the air felt warm and dry. The sun shone in my eyes as I clomped down the steps in my jeans and cowboy boots.

The street was wet, as if it had just been washed, and some shopkeepers were sweeping in front of their stores. At the corner an Oriental man at the vegetable stand was putting out boxes of blueberries. Green grapes, apples, and oranges shone in the sunlight, and there were bouquets of tulips and roses next to the vegetables. I felt elated looking at it all.

A fat, dark-haired lady was sitting in a doorway across the street from the vegetable stand. The sign on her window said Palms and Fortunes. She motioned for me to come over. I shook my head and kept going.

When I got to the next corner, I was waiting for the light to change when I glanced at the guy standing next to me. He was filthy with matted hair and no shoes. I looked anxiously back at the light. "Hey," the guy said, and he reached out to touch my arm.

I turned and hurried back up the street. I charged around the corner and rushed to my dad's building. I stood at the top of the stoop and watched the corner for a few minutes to make sure the guy hadn't followed me.

I was about to head out again when I noticed a boy about sixteen or seventeen crossing the street toward the building. He had a couple of books under his arm. He climbed the steps without looking at me; I stepped aside so he could go in the front door. A minute later he came back out, still carrying the books. He passed me again and sat on the bottom step. I stared down at his blond head.

He must have felt my nervous presence hovering above him, because he turned and looked up at me. I glanced at my watch as if I were waiting for somebody.

"You live here?" His voice was deep.

I looked down at him, blinking as if I hadn't realized he was there. "What?"

"You live here?" He had straight hair sort of parted in the middle, and a long serious face. His skin was tanned and smooth.

"I'm visiting my father."

A slow smile spread across his face. "Oh, where are y'all from?" he said in a mock southern accent.

My face flushed. "North Carolina."

"Oh, really?" he said, looking serious again. "Who are you visiting?"

"Uh—Richard Murray," I said. Damn my red face. The guy didn't say anything. He just stared at me. I held on to the railing and sat down on the top step, trying to gain some control.

"What's your name?" he said.

I didn't want to tell him my name. If he thought my accent was funny, he'd die when he heard my name.

"You haven't got a name?" he said.

"It's Blue," I said softly.

He nodded as if he weren't surprised at all. "Blue—like your eyes?"

I smiled a little. "Yes."

He kept staring at me with a thoughtful, sexy expression. I wondered if I was more appealing to New York boys than North Carolina boys. I cleared my throat and said, "What's your name?"

"Nathaniel."

What a beautiful name, I thought. But I just nodded. I didn't trust my voice.

"How long are you visiting your father, Blue?"

"Two weeks." I hoped he was thinking of asking me out.

"You like New York?"

"Yeah, it's nice." I was being so boring.

"Would you like to go to the movies while you're here?"

I nodded and shrugged at the same time. I didn't know if he meant go with him or just go to some movies while I was in New York.

"You want to go later today?"

I nodded and shrugged again.

Nathaniel stood up and kicked out his leg to get his khaki pants to fall into place. I was afraid I'd been too nonchalant and now he was just going to leave without asking me out at all. But in the next second he said, "Okay, I'll call you later."

I smiled and felt my face heating up again. I couldn't even remember my dad's number. "I'll have to go inside and get the number," I said.

"It's okay. I know it. I know your dad," he said.

"You do?"

"Yeah."

"How?"

"He and my mom used to go out together."

"Oh." I wondered if his mother was the actress-cook.

"Could you give him these books, please? He lent them to me a couple of months ago. I'm bringing them back—that's why I came over."

I stood up and walked down the steps to him. He

was taller than I was when we were standing side by side. "Is your mother's name Annie?" I said.

He nodded. "Yeah. Well, I'll call you."

"Okay," I said.

"See you later." He smiled, then turned and headed up the street with his hands in his pockets.

" 'Bye," I said. I couldn't believe this had just happened. I'd waited fifteen years for a date, and in just ten seconds practically I'd met a beautiful boy and he'd asked me out!

I was smiling like an idiot as I turned and started to rush up the steps. I caught myself and straightened my shoulders and stepped gracefully up to the door—just in case Nathaniel might be looking back at me.

16

When I got inside my dad's apartment, I sat down at the kitchen table and tried to remember exactly how Nathaniel had looked. But just like in a dream, I couldn't remember the details of his appearance. I lay down on Dad's bed and for a long time kept trying to conjure up Nathaniel's face, but I couldn't get it.

I was still lying there, staring at the ceiling, when I heard Dad's key turn in the lock. I jumped off the bed to greet him. But as soon as he stepped into the apartment, I knew something was wrong.

"Hi," I said.

"Hi, babe," he said. His lips were sealed together in a little smile.

"How did it go?"

"Uh—not very well." He put his briefcase on the kitchen table and started taking off his tie.

"Did something bad happen?"

"Well, I'm afraid we didn't agree on very much," he said.

"Why? What did he say?"

"He just wanted to make some changes I didn't like. So"—he took a deep breath—"I told him we'd better forget the whole thing." He put his tie on his bureau and sat down on the end of the bed.

"So your play won't be done off-off-Broadway?" I said.

"Not with these people. . . ."

"Oh, dammit."

"It's okay," he said. "So I'm not a playwright after all. I'm a cabdriver. It's not the end of the world, right?"

"No. You're not a cabdriver! You're a writer. You are!"

"Right."

"I'm so mad. I wanted your play to get done!"

"Hmm. Me too," he said.

"It's not fair! You're a great writer. You shouldn't be driving a cab. I hate it!"

"I know, bluebird. Thanks. Look," he said, "don't tell Mackie about this, okay?"

"Of course I won't tell her! I wouldn't tell anybody. They wouldn't understand how brave you are."

"Brave, huh?"

"I mean it—you're trying to be creative and you wrote all those plays and you struggle—you're the bravest person I know!"

"You think so, huh?"

"Yes."

He smiled. "What do *you* know?"

"Lots."

"I wish you were right about me."

"I am."

He went to the sink and poured himself a glass of water. "So what did you do while I was gone?" he said, turning to me.

"I took a walk."

"Yeah? How was it?"

"Okay. I met someone you know," I said.

"Who?"

"Nathaniel."

"Nat Lawrence? How in the hell did you meet him?" Dad said.

"He was bringing back some books you'd lent him." I pointed to the books on his dresser.

"Oh, right. How did he like them?"

"I didn't ask him."

"Oh. Did he say how Annie was doing?"

"No," I said.

"Huh. Well . . . did you have breakfast yet?" Dad said.

"No."

"Then do you feel like going out again? We could have lunch together somewhere."

"Sure. I'd love to."

"Good," he said, and he put his glass in the sink. "Then what should we do?"

I was relieved that he seemed to be getting over his bad mood. "What about going to the park?" I said.

"Oh, right. Why not?"

The phone rang. Dad picked it up. "Hello. . . .

Oh, hi, Nat. I got the books. Did you like them? . . . Good. . . . What? Oh . . . yeah, sure. . . ." He looked at me quizzically. "It's for you," he said.

I could feel my heart start pounding as I took the receiver. "Hello?" I said.

"Hi, it's me, Nathaniel." His voice sounded mature over the phone. Or maybe it was just the fact that he didn't have a southern accent that made him sound that way.

"I checked the *Voice*," he said. "That scary Spielberg movie is playing at the Waverly. There's a two-o'clock show. You want to go?"

"Um, just a minute—I'd better ask." I covered the mouthpiece. "He wants me to go to the movies with him this afternoon!"

"He does?" Dad said. "Now?"

"Yeah. Do you want me to tell him I can't?"

"No, babe, you can go. Of course you can go. . . ."

"Well, okay, I guess I can," I said to Nathaniel.

"Good, I'll come over and get you around one fifteen."

"All right."

"See you then," he said. " 'Bye."

" 'Bye." I hung up and looked at my dad. He got up and started taking the money out of his pockets and putting it on top of his bureau.

"You sure it's okay if I go out with him?" I said.

"Sure. He's a nice kid." He didn't look at me.

"Well, can we still go get some lunch first?" I said.

"What time do you have to go?"

"One fifteen."

"Well, then, no—it's twelve thirty. You don't have time to go anywhere. Why don't you just run down-stairs and get a sandwich or something?"

"Where?"

"There's a deli downstairs," he said, still not look-ing at me.

I was starting to feel awful. "Are you mad?" I asked.

"No."

"You seem mad."

"I'm not mad."

"I'd rather have lunch with you than go out with that guy. I wasn't thinking . . ."

He looked at me.

"I wish I hadn't said yes. I don't even know him! But what can I do now?" I said.

"Well, you want to call him back and tell him you've changed your mind?"

"Yeah," I said, picking up the phone. "I'll tell him I don't feel well or something. What's his number?"

Dad told me Nathaniel's number. I dialed, but there was no answer. "He's not there!" I said. "What are we going to do?"

"Okay, calm down," Dad said. "This is silly. Just go ahead and go out with him. It's fine, really. I'll be fine, okay? Look—I'll go down to the deli and get you some lunch."

"I don't care about eating," I said.

"Oh, come on. How about a turkey sandwich?" he said as he headed to the door.

"Okay, that's fine."

After he left, I slumped down onto the bed. I felt

miserable now about going out with Nathaniel and leaving my dad.

A few minutes later Dad came back from the deli with a little white bag. "Okay. I got a turkey sandwich, a Coke, and what else? A limp pickle." He pulled everything out of the bag, then popped the top off the Coke can and stuck a straw in it.

I sat at the table and picked at my sandwich. Dad sat across from me smoking a cigarette.

"Why don't you ever eat?" I said.

He shrugged.

"You should eat," I said. "You're real skinny."

"Yeah, I know."

"Well, how come you don't eat?"

"I'm never hungry," he said.

"I'm not very hungry either." I pushed my sandwich and its wrapping away from me.

"Oh, c'mon," Dad said. "You should have lunch—"

"I know. So should you." Neither of us said anything for a moment.

"What are you going to do while I'm gone?" I said.

He didn't answer. He was just staring past me smoking his cigarette.

"Dad?"

"What?" He blinked at me.

"What are you going to do while I'm gone?"

"Well . . ." He looked around the room. "I don't really know."

I felt a little scared. This was the way he had sometimes acted at home—as if he were far away. "You going to stay here?" I said.

He shrugged.

"You don't know?" I said.

He just stared at me.

"What are you going to do?" I said sharply.

"I don't know, Blue!"

"Jeez!" I said, getting out of my chair.

"Where are you going?"

"I have a date? You remember I had a date?"

He nodded.

"Well, I have to get dressed for it." I went into my little room and rummaged through my garment bag looking for the right thing to wear. Finally I jerked out my new crepe dress.

When I walked back into the kitchen, Dad was still sitting in his chair, exactly as I had left him. He looked up at me. "Oh, Blue," he said in a quiet voice.

"What's wrong?" I said.

"You're a vision."

"Do you like my new dress?"

"Yeah, you're a vision," he said again.

"Thanks." I wished so much that the two of us were going out someplace together now, but before I could tell him that, the buzzer rang.

17

Dad got up from the table and went over to the intercom. "Come on up, Nat," he said, pressing a button on the box. He unlocked the lock and sat back down.

"Dad, I wish—" I said.

"No, come on, I'm okay," he said quickly.

A few seconds later there was a tap on the door. "Come in," Dad called. "It's open."

Nathaniel pushed open the door. He was dressed in the same khakis and T-shirt as this morning. Now I remembered how he looked—wonderful. "Hi, Richard," he said.

Dad nodded without saying anything.

"Hi, Blue," Nathaniel said. "Wow, you're all dressed up."

"It's just a dress," I said a little defensively. "Am I too dressed up?"

"No, no, you look great," Nathaniel said.

None of us said anything for a couple of seconds. "Well . . . ready to go?" Nathaniel asked.

"What's the rush?" Dad said coldly.

"There'll probably be a line," Nathaniel said.

"Oh."

"I have to get my bag," I mumbled as I headed into my room. I felt terrible. I didn't understand why Dad and Nathaniel weren't being nicer to each other. I grabbed my bag and hurried back into the room. "I'm ready," I said, without looking at either of them.

Dad opened the door for us and put his hand on my shoulder. " 'Bye," he said.

"I'll be back soon," I said.

"See you, Richard," Nathaniel said.

"Right." Dad closed the door behind us.

I walked ahead of Nathaniel down the stairs and out of the building. I ignored him when he fell into step beside me. I knew it wasn't fair, but I was mad at him for making me desert my dad.

"This way," Nathaniel said, directing me around the corner. "It's supposed to be a pretty good movie," he said.

"I know."

"That's the theater up ahead," he said. As we headed toward the marquee, I wondered if I should pay for my own ticket. I remembered Susan had said she always paid for herself on the first date. I zipped open my bag and pulled out my wallet.

"Hey, I'll get the tickets," Nathaniel said when we got to the window.

"No. I'll get mine," I said.

"That's okay—"

"No, no, I want to," I said, and I gave the ticket lady my money.

"Okay, if you say so," Nathaniel said. Then he bought his own ticket and followed me into the red-carpeted lobby.

"You want some popcorn?" he said.

"No, thank you."

"I think I'll get some." He stepped up to the counter and ordered his popcorn. I went over to a movie poster in a glass case and pretended to study it. I could see my reflection in the glass. I *was* too dressed up, I thought. I wished I could go back home to my dad's.

Nathaniel came over and stood beside me. He started digging into his popcorn box and stuffing popcorn into his mouth. I turned away from him and watched people walk through the lobby.

"What are you looking at?" he said.

"Nothing."

"Well, why don't you look at me?"

I was surprised at his directness. I turned around and looked at him. There was salt around his lips and his face looked flushed in the rosy light of the lobby.

"There. That's better," he said. He took another handful of popcorn. I turned away again.

"Hey . . ." he said. I looked back at him. He swallowed, then said, "Why'd you go away again?"

"What do you mean?"

"You seem angry."

"I'm not angry."

"I'm starting to get the feeling you'd rather not be here." He was starting to sound angry himself.

"Well, I guess I don't have much choice now," I said.

"Oh. Well, yes, you do have a choice," he said. "You can go right now. I'll give you your money back. Here—hold this. . . ." He handed me his popcorn box and took out his wallet.

"No, don't," I said. I looked around to see if anyone was watching us. This was horrible.

"Here—" He took his popcorn back. "Here's five dollars. You didn't lose a thing. You can go now."

"I don't want to leave," I said.

"Well, you obviously don't want to be here with me," he said.

"Yes, I do," I said.

"What made you change your mind?"

"I didn't change my mind. I really do want to be here with you. It's just that—well, my dad wanted me to spend some time with him this afternoon."

Nathaniel stared at me for a few seconds, then he put his five dollars back in his pocket. "I'd like you to stay," he said.

"Thanks."

He held out his box of popcorn to me. "You want some?"

I nodded and took a few pieces. He took another handful. I took some more and we chomped together, standing close to each other.

"Where do you like to sit?" he said.

"I guess in the middle."

"Me too. You go to movies in North Carolina?"

"No," I said. "We don't have movies in the South yet."

"I didn't think so," he said. "What do you do for entertainment?"

"We go square dancing and have quilting parties. You know, like in *Gone With the Wind.*"

"Sounds neat," he said. We smiled at each other. I looked him straight in the eye; he had nice green eyes.

"I really like your dress," he said. "You look elegant."

"Thank you. So do you."

He smiled, then he took the last handful of popcorn and threw the box away. He brushed his hands off. "Ready?" he said.

"Yes."

He casually reached for my hand and led me into the auditorium. My hand in his felt greasy and grainy, but I held on tightly as we walked down the dark aisle.

18

The first part of the movie was funny, and Nathaniel and I laughed together. When it started getting scary, he took my hand, and at one unexpected scary part he yelled and grabbed my whole arm.

When the movie was over, we sat holding hands and watched through the very end of the credits. Almost everyone else was gone when we finally stood up to leave.

"Are you still scared?" Nathaniel said.

"A little. How about you?"

"I was never scared."

"Oh, yes, you were!" I said, shaking his arm.

He pretended to strangle me. "No, I wasn't."

I laughed. "Okay, you weren't! You weren't!"

"What do you want to do now?" he said as we came out of the theater into the bright sunlight.

I wanted to stay with him, but I pictured my dad waiting for me back at the apartment. "I guess I should go back home," I said.

"Right now?"

"Well, my dad's expecting me."

"Are you still worried about him?" he said gently.

"I'm not worried about him. It's just that he wasn't expecting me to stay out all day."

Nathaniel looked at his watch. "C'mon, it's only four thirty. Why don't you call him and tell him we're going to stop off for a Coke or something?"

"Well, I'd really like to, but I better go back. He had kind of a bad morning and I want to see how he's doing." I also didn't want Dad to think I'd rather be with Nathaniel than him.

"Well, I think your dad would probably be okay, but it's your choice. Come on, I'll walk you home." Nathaniel put his hands in his pockets and we started down the sidewalk. I couldn't tell if he was mad at me or just acting cool.

When we got to my dad's building, I realized I'd left my keys upstairs in my jeans. "Oh darn," I said. "I forgot my keys. Do you know how to work this intercom thing?"

"Of course." Nathaniel stepped past me into the hallway. "First, you find his name," he said. "Second, you locate the button next to his name. Third, you push that button."

I giggled.

"Now, miraculously, your father's voice will come over that speaker," Nathaniel said.

We waited, grinning at each other. Nothing happened. "Whoops," Nathaniel said. He pushed the button again. "I guess he went out," he said after a moment.

"He's not there?"

"No. Hey, now's our chance—why don't we get that Coke while you wait for him to get back?"

"Where do you think he went?" I said.

"I don't know, but I wouldn't worry about it. I'm sure he's okay. C'mon."

"Well . . . is there a place to go near here?" I said.

"Sure. We could go to the restaurant where my mother cooks."

"It's near here?"

"Yeah, it's right around the corner on Bleecker Street. It's two minutes away."

"Oh. Is your mom there now?" I said.

"Yeah, I think she'd really like to meet you."

"She would?"

"Yeah. How do you feel about meeting her?" he said.

I wasn't sure how I felt about meeting her. "A little weird," I said.

Nathaniel took my hand. "Why? Because she used to go with your dad?"

I nodded.

"Come on." He smiled. "She's really a nice person."

"Well, okay. But just for a little while."

Nathaniel and I walked around the corner to Bleecker Street, and he led me into a white brick building with a green awning. No one was inside the restaurant except a blond guy washing glasses behind the bar.

"Hi, Doug," Nathaniel said.

"Hi, Nat. How's it going?"

"Okay. This is Blue Murray. Blue, this is Doug." Doug and I said hi to each other.

"Can I put a tape in?" Nathaniel said.

"Sure," Doug said.

Nathaniel picked out a tape from behind the bar and put it into a tape machine. A sexy drumbeat started playing. Nathaniel came around and sat on the barstool next to me.

"What can I get you?" Doug said.

"Just a Sprite," Nathaniel said. Then he turned to me and said, "How about you?"

"A Sprite's fine."

A woman in a blue-checked apron came out the kitchen door. She had curly brown hair and rosy cheeks. "Hi, shortie," she said to Nathaniel. "I thought it was you when I heard that music."

"Hi, Mom," he said.

Annie looked younger than I'd imagined. She had jeans on under her apron, and it didn't look like she was wearing any makeup.

"Could I get a Beck's please, Doug? Thanks," she said. "Where have you been?" she asked Nathaniel.

"The movies."

She took her beer from Doug, then walked over to us.

I turned and stared at the liquor bottles behind the bar and sipped my Sprite. I felt nervous about meeting her.

"Guess who this is." Nathaniel leaned back so his mother could see me better.

"Who?" She smiled.

He held up an imaginary microphone and gestured to me. "It's *Blue Murray!*" he said like an emcee. I laughed, embarrassed.

"Richard's daughter?"

"Yep. It's Blue. She's up visiting from North Carolina."

"Oh, my! Hi, Blue," she said. "I'm Annie Lawrence."

"Hi," I said.

"When did you get here? How did you two meet? This is remarkable!"

"I came yesterday."

"I was taking the books back to Richard today—" Nathaniel said.

"What books?"

"You know, those Faulkner books he lent me. And Blue was sitting on the front steps, and we met and then we went to the movies."

"Boy, you move fast, kid," Annie said to Nathaniel. "I've heard so much about you, Blue," she said. "Richard talked about you all the time. How long will you be here?"

"Two weeks."

"That's wonderful. Now, don't let Nat play the city slicker and lead you astray," she said.

"Mom—" Nathaniel said.

"Only kidding. You have any cigarettes?" she asked him.

"I quit, remember?" he said.

"Oh, that's right. I guess I'll have to start buying my own."

"Or quit," he said coolly.

She took a swipe at him. I giggled. Annie acted more like Nathaniel's kid sister than his mother.

"So, how's your dad?" she asked me.

"He's fine," I said. "I think he was really glad to see me."

"Yeah . . . I'm sure he was. It's great that you got to come up here." She smiled at me. "Welcome to New York."

"Thanks." I smiled back at her. I liked her.

"Hey—what's the news about Richard's play?" she said.

"What play?" Nathaniel said.

"You know, the one Tom's going to direct," she said. "Weren't they going to have a meeting about it today?" she asked me.

"Yes, but I don't think it went very well," I said.

"What?"

"Well, I don't think your friend's going to direct it anymore."

"Oh, no! Why not?" Annie seemed genuinely upset.

"I don't know. He and my dad didn't agree about some things."

"Oh, no, that's too bad! Oh, I hope that didn't disappoint Richard too much."

"No, I think he's okay," I said.

"Oh, I know he's okay—it's just that he has such a problem getting over disappointments. He gets so down. Damn! Why didn't it work out with Tom? I thought the two of them would get along great!"

"Mom, relax," Nathaniel said.

"Well, you know how he is!" she said.

Nathaniel looked at me uncomfortably.

"I'm sorry, Blue," Annie said. "I get carried away. But I know your dad can get so depressed about these kinds of things."

"He's fine now," I said. I couldn't stand hearing her talk about him this way. She was sounding like my mother.

"I'm glad," she said. "I really care about him. I just hope he doesn't give up—"

"I told you he's fine." I looked away from her. There was silence for a moment.

Nathaniel looked at his watch. "Hey, you want to go?" he said.

I nodded.

"Oh, don't go!" Annie said.

"Blue's got to get back. Richard's expecting her," Nathaniel said. "I'll walk you back," he said to me.

"No, that's okay. It's just around the corner, right? Really, it's okay."

"You sure?"

"Yeah." I stood up.

"Blue . . ." Annie rested her hand on my arm. "I'm glad Richard's fine. I really am."

"I know. Thanks." I backed toward the door. " 'Bye."

" 'Bye," Nathaniel said.

I pushed open the door and left the restaurant. I hurried around the corner to my dad's street. I felt terrible now for being away from him this long. Annie had made him sound so fragile—I hated that.

I ran up the steps of Dad's building and tried his buzzer. There was no answer. I went back out and sat on the steps and watched anxiously for him.

I'd only been waiting a few minutes when I saw him round the corner with a large shopping bag in his arms. I jumped up and ran to him. "Where were you?" I cried.

"I'm sorry. When did the movie get out? Were you waiting long?"

"No . . . no, not too long. Where did you go?" I said as we walked to his building.

"I went shopping for a few things," he said. "Trying to make our lives a little more decent." He laughed.

I was so relieved. He didn't seem depressed at all. "What kind of things did you get?" I said.

He stopped and peered at me over the shopping bag. "I got you a pillow," he said.

"You did?"

"Yep." We headed up the steps together and he fumbled in his pocket for his keys.

"What else?" I said.

"Many little things to make us merry." He smiled and held the door open for me.

19

When we got inside the apartment, Dad put his shopping bag on the bed. I sat down next to it, and like a little kid tried to see what was inside. "All I see is a pillow," I said.

"No—wait," Dad said. He took his money out of his pockets and put it on top of his bureau. Then he came back over to the shopping bag and pulled out the pillow. "See—one genuine, authentic store-bought pillow," he said, handing it to me.

"Thanks." I hugged it and watched as he reached into the shopping bag and pulled out a little brown sack. "Coffee—Mocha Java—the real thing, not instant."

"Oh, boy," I said.

"And"—he reached into the bag again—"Cards—in case we need something to do on a rainy day." He tossed a pack of playing cards onto the bed. "And—homemade chocolate." He held out two bars of chocolate wrapped in purple waxed paper. "Smell them," he said.

I took a whiff of the chocolate, then fell over backward on the bed. "I'm dead," I said, my eyes closed.

I heard him laugh. I opened my eyes and looked up at him.

"I'm sorry I acted like a jerk," he said.

"When?" I sat up. "You didn't act like a jerk."

"Yeah, I did. . . . Did you and Nat have a good time at the movies?"

I nodded.

"Good, I'm glad." He kept staring at me. "Don't give up on me, Blue, please," he said.

"What do you mean?"

"I mean you should probably turn your back on me like everyone else. But please don't."

I laughed a little. "I won't, Dad."

He put the chocolate down on his bedside table. "Okay, you want to help me make this coffee?" He picked up the brown coffee sack and headed over to the stove.

"Sure." I followed him and sat down at the kitchen table. I watched as he turned on the fire underneath the kettle. Then he took down a porcelain coffeepot from his shelf and filled a paper cone with a couple of spoonfuls of the fresh coffee grounds. I could smell it from where I sat. "It smells good," I said.

"It does, doesn't it?" He lit a cigarette and turned to face me.

"Dad, have you thought much about your play?" I said.

"What's there to think about?"

"I just wondered if you were still upset about it."

"No—it's no use," he said.

"What's no use?"

"Messing with it anymore." He stared at the wall and took a few drags on his cigarette.

"Well—maybe you should show it to somebody else," I said.

The kettle started to whistle. Dad poured the steaming water into the coffee cone; then he put the kettle back on the stove and turned to me. "Do you know how many untalented people there are in New York trying to make it?" he said.

I shook my head.

"I know at least a dozen," he said. "They hang out at the bar where Annie works. They drive cabs from the same garage I used to. They do all the things I do. I'm one of them, Blue." He poured coffee into our two cups and set mine on the table. "I just used to have trouble accepting it."

"No, you're talented," I said. "You just need to believe in yourself."

"Yeah, right," he said.

"Dad, I think believing in yourself is the main thing you need to do. I think—" I started to say more, but the phone interrupted me. "Darn," I said.

It rang again, but Dad didn't make a move to answer it. When it rang a third time, I went over and picked it up. "Hello?" I said.

"Blue?" It was my mother. I couldn't believe her bad timing.

"Oh, hi, Mom."

"How are you?" she said.

I didn't answer her. I glanced over at my dad. He was leaning against the sink with his arms crossed, staring at me.

"Blue?" Mom said.

I looked away from Dad and said, "What?"

"What's wrong?" she said.

"Nothing's wrong."

"Why didn't you answer me?"

"What did you say?" I said.

"I just wanted to know how everything is going."

"Fine."

There was a pause, then Mom said, "Blue, can I speak to Richard?"

"He's not here," I said. I felt like I shouldn't put my dad on the phone now. Mom would just make him feel worse.

"Where is he? Did he leave you alone?" she said.

"No, I mean he's here, but he's in the bathroom taking a shower. Then we're going out to dinner," I said.

"Oh. How's he doing?"

"He's doing fine."

"What did you do today?"

"Oh, we took it easy. Mom—I better go. I have to get dressed. We're leaving as soon as he gets out of the shower."

"Are you sure everything's all right, honey? You're still having a good time?" she said.

"Yes, yes, I am. I'll call you every couple of days, okay, Mom?"

"Okay, honey. . . ."

"I'll talk to you later." I tried to sound cheerful.
" 'Bye now."

" 'Bye, Blue."

I hung up and looked at my dad.

"Why did you lie?" he said in a quiet voice.

"I didn't think you'd want to talk to her right
now."

"How come?"

"I thought— I don't know! Did you want to talk
to her?"

"You thought I couldn't handle it?"

"No. I didn't think that."

Dad crushed out his cigarette and stared blankly
at the ashtray. He looked totally defeated.

"I didn't think that," I said again.

"I know. It's Mackie—she thinks I'm sick."

"No, she doesn't. Why do you say that?"

He shook his head.

I went over to him. "She doesn't think you're *sick*.
She just wants a different life than you do."

"What kind of life does she want, Blue?"

"You know—the club and stuff."

"Is she dating anyone now?" he said.

"Well, not *dating*." I sat down at the table. "She
plays tennis sometimes with this guy named Bob."

"What's he like?"

"Oh, you know, kind of a businessman—real
straight and boring."

"Does she see him a lot?"

"No, I don't think so. Dad—Mom just has different values from you. She doesn't understand writers
or artists. She's so straight."

He didn't say anything.

"I don't think you ever belonged in Layette," I said. "I don't belong there either, really. I'm more like you than anyone else. In Layette no one takes the time to appreciate things like good books or poetry. People there never write plays. That was a great thing you did—whether you believe it or not!"

He shook his head.

"It *was* a great thing!" I said. "Not everyone can write a play, Dad. They can't!"

"Okay, okay." He smiled a little and held up his hand.

I stared at the cracked plastic tablecloth in front of me. "You know what?" I said. "I wish you could just explain to Mom that you're marching to a different drummer than everybody else."

He laughed. It was a real laugh.

"What's so funny?" I said.

"Nothing." He sat down at the table and took my hands and clasped them between his. "You're a bluebird, you know that?"

I smiled at him, then nodded. "You want to go out and do something tonight?" I said.

"Sure. What do you want to do?"

"I don't know. Maybe we should go get something to eat." I was starving—I hadn't really eaten much since I'd been here.

"Oh, then I know what we can do," he said. "I'll take you to Maria's!"

"Who's Maria?"

He laughed. "No, no, it's a little café near here."

"Oh." I laughed too. "Do they have good food?"

"They have terrific soup and sandwiches."

"Great, let's do it!" I said.

Dad went to his bureau and got his money off the top. I felt a great wave of love for him as I watched him drop his change into his pockets. I'd seen him do this so many times in my life. He turned to me and said, "Ready?"

"Yep." I got up and crossed to the bed and got my purse.

"Hey—grab those and we'll take them for dessert," Dad said.

"What?"

He pointed to the chocolate he'd bought us, on his bedside table.

"Oh, that's a great idea!" I said.

It felt good to be outside. The sun was going down, turning the sky a soft peach color. We walked half a block, then I stopped. The sound of a horn was coming from a ground-floor apartment. "Wait—what's that music?" I said.

"A clarinet," Dad said. "Some poor turkey's practicing to be the next Benny Goodman."

I giggled. "It sounds nice." I felt like we were in a movie as we stood listening to the guy play. A breeze blew the curtain of his window. We couldn't see him—I could just see a white brick wall and a hanging fern moving in the breeze.

The café was only a block away, but I made us stop two more times before we got there—once outside a bakery, so we could smell the fresh bread baking, and once to watch a magician doing card tricks on the sidewalk.

At Maria's we sat at a lantern-lit table on a back terrace. Dad and I ordered bean soup and ham-and-cheese sandwiches. A man and woman were playing the guitar and flute on the patio.

When I finished eating, I turned toward the music. It was wonderful, all this atmosphere. I started thinking about Nathaniel. I hoped he wasn't mad at me for leaving the restaurant so abruptly. I imagined the two of us listening to this music together. I turned back to my dad. "I love this place," I said.

"Good."

I pointed to a moth fluttering around the lamp on our table. "Know what I read?" I said.

"What?"

"That when light strikes a moth's eyes, it causes its muscles to start to turn. So whether he likes it or not, his whole body gets turned toward the light. He can't control it. And sometimes they get burned up like that."

Dad smiled. "Sounds pretty grim."

"Yeah, it does. But it's interesting, isn't it? I'm collecting facts on insects."

"Hmm. Insects are important," he said. "Details about anything are important if you want to be a writer."

"I'd like to be a writer," I said. "Or an actress."

"An actress, huh? Okay, I'll write plays and you can act in them," he said.

"Oh, that sounds great!" I said. "I'd love that."

"You would, huh?" His eyes seemed to be sparkling as he looked at me.

"Yeah," I said.

We listened to the music a little while longer; then Dad put out his cigarette and said, "Ready, bluebird?"

"If you are," I said.

On the way home we ate our chocolate. We stopped and listened to a black man playing his guitar and singing "Hey, Mr. Tambourine Man." He jerked his head from side to side and almost shouted out the words. It was haunting. Dad had his arm around me as we listened. When the song was over, he dropped a couple of dollars in the guy's guitar case.

When we got back to the apartment, Dad sat down on his bed. He'd been very quiet since we'd left the café.

"I had a really good time tonight," I said.

"Good." He squinted thoughtfully at me; I couldn't tell what he was thinking.

"Did you?" I said.

"Yeah, yeah." He nodded and smiled.

"Are you going to bed now?" I said.

"No, I'm a little wired," he said. "I may read for a while or something. You go ahead."

We stared at each other for a couple of seconds, then he picked up my pillow. "Here—take your genuine store-bought pillow. . . ." He tossed the pillow to me.

"Good night, angel," he said.

"Good night, Dad."

I went into my room. Without turning on the overhead light, I changed into my nightgown and lay down on my cot. I could hear loud music coming from somewhere outside, then it faded away. I loved being here. Everything seemed so dramatic and intense. More had happened to me in just one day in New York than in a whole year practically in Layette.

20

I slept late the next morning. When I woke up, the apartment was quiet. I sat up in bed and called out to Dad, but there was no answer.

I went into his room. His bed was made, and there was a note on the kitchen table that said, "Going out for a while. Didn't want to wake you. Be back soon. Love, Dad."

I was so disappointed. I wished he'd gotten me up so we could have gone out together. I pictured him having breakfast in a café or something without me. I went to the window and stared down at the corner, hoping he'd come back home soon.

The phone rang, startling me. I hurried to it and picked up the receiver. "Hello?" I said.

"Hi, Blue. It's Nathaniel."

"Oh, hi!" I was surprised to hear his voice.

"How are you?" he said.

"I'm fine."

"What are you doing today?" he said.

"I don't know. My dad's gone out somewhere. What are you doing?"

"Well, I wanted to know if you could go for a walk."

"Yeah, sure, I'd love to."

"Great. I'll be over in fifteen minutes, okay?"

"Okay," I said." 'Bye."

I hung up and rushed into my room. I got out my new yellow painter's pants and green T-shirt, then I pinned up my hair and put on some makeup. When I was dressed and ready to go, I scribbled a note to my dad in case he came back and I wasn't here. I just told him I was going out for a walk; I didn't mention Nathaniel. For a little joke I signed it, "Love always, Blue"—that's how I'd signed all my letters to him since he'd left home.

I sat by the window and looked down at the street. When I saw Nathaniel turn the corner, I hurried to the door and waited by the intercom till the buzzer rang. "I'm coming," I yelled into the box, then I grabbed my purse and keys and ran downstairs.

Nathaniel was standing by the curb with his hands in his pockets. He was wearing a pair of faded jeans and a white shirt with the sleeves rolled up. He smiled when he saw me.

"Hi," I said.

"Hi. You look very nice."

"Thank you. So do you," I said. "Where do you want to go?"

"Let's just walk," he said.

"Okay."

The concrete sparkled with sunlight as we headed up the sidewalk.

"I wasn't sure you'd want to see me today," Nathaniel said.

"Why not?" I pretended I didn't know what he was talking about.

"I was afraid my mom had upset you."

"She didn't upset me."

"Then why did you leave so quickly yesterday?" He stopped and stared at me.

"Well, I guess she did upset me a little," I said.

"Why? Because she got carried away about your dad?"

"Yes."

"Well, she's a little hyper," he said.

"I know, but I thought she said some things about him that were kind of negative," I said.

"Like what?"

"Well, you know, about how depressed he got and stuff like that. It doesn't matter . . ." I looked away from him. I didn't want to talk about this now. He didn't know about how Annie's attitude had reminded me of my mother's, about how everyone back home always acted like something was really wrong with my dad.

"It matters if it makes you mad at me," Nathaniel said.

"I was never mad at you," I said. "I was just a little mad at your mother. She was acting like she knew more about my dad than I did."

"Well, she does know him in ways that you don't," he said softly.

"Oh, wow," I said, turning away from him.

"I didn't mean that like it sounded—" he said.

"I think I know him a lot better than she does," I said quickly. "I mean even though he's not living at home anymore, we write to each other."

"I know. I heard some of your letters."

"What?"

"Richard read some of your letters to me and Mom."

"Oh." So Nathaniel and Annie had been the ones he'd read my letters to.

"I liked them," he said. "I've never known a girl who wrote letters like that. That's why I wanted to meet you."

"You wanted to meet me before I came up here?"

"Yeah. I even thought about writing to you—like pen pals."

"That would have been weird," I said, laughing a little.

"Yeah." Nathaniel stopped to tie one of his sneakers. I stared at his tanned, slender arms. I tried to remember what kind of things I might have written that had made him like me so much. "I don't remember much about what I wrote in those letters," I said.

Nathaniel straightened up. "Well, for one thing, you sounded like you missed Richard a lot," he said.

"I did—he made my life not so boring. I hate living down there."

"Your life is boring?"

"Down there it is."

"Have you ever been in love?" he said.

"What's that got to do with anything?"

"Life probably wouldn't be so boring if you fell in love," he said softly.

Suddenly I felt short of breath. "I don't know," I said. "I never go out with anyone down there or anything."

"How come?"

"I don't know." I wasn't about to talk about being too tall and skinny.

"Are you afraid?" he said.

"What's there to be afraid of?" I said, hoping he wasn't about to confront me with stuff about sex.

"I don't know," he said. "Just afraid."

"I'm not sure," I said. I stared at him. He had the sexiest expression on his face. "Do you—do you want to walk around some more?" I said.

He smiled and then looked up the street. "Sure," he said. "I guess we could go to Washington Square. You want to?"

"Okay."

He led me across a busy avenue; then we walked a couple of blocks till we came within sight of a tree-filled park. Nathaniel touched my arm. "When we go in there," he said, "don't pay any attention to the drug dealers. Just ignore them."

"Is it safe?" I said.

"Sure. You just have to be a little street smart," he said, and he took my hand. He was so different from the guys in my high school, I thought. I could hardly wait to tell Susan about him.

We entered a large square full of trees and benches and grassy open spaces. Old men were playing chess on concrete tables. Some little kids ran squealing past us, chasing each other. We laughed and looked back at them over our shoulders. This park seemed safe enough, I thought.

But no sooner had I thought that than some weird-looking guy stepped in front of us saying, "Good smoke, good smoke."

I grabbed Nathaniel's arm. "Ignore him," he said, and we kept going.

I noticed another couple of weird guys advancing toward us, and I started to stop. "Come on," Nathaniel said, and he moved me around them as one of the guys said, "Good smoke, uppers . . ."

"Okay?" Nathaniel said when we'd gotten past them.

I nodded. But suddenly a lady with a towel wrapped around her head started yelling at us. Then she turned and ranted at a tree. "What's she doing?" I said.

"Don't worry about it."

I looked back at her. It made me a little sick to watch her.

"You want to sit somewhere?" Nathaniel said, pulling my arm gently to get my attention. I nodded, and he led me to a wooden bench across from a big fountain.

"What happens to people like that woman who was talking to herself back there?" I said.

"What do you mean?" Nathaniel said.

"Who takes care of them?"

"I don't know—they seem to take care of themselves," Nathaniel said. "There's a crazy drunk guy who stands all day in a phone booth on our corner. Every day he has on a different set of clothes. So he must go home somewhere and change and then come back and stand in the phone booth."

"That's awful," I said.

"Oh, it's not so bad. I'd rather live in a phone booth than a lot of other places. It's peaceful and you could receive calls—"

"Oh, you're crazy," I said, punching his arm.

"Thanks a lot."

"You deserve it," I said.

"You should kiss me instead of hit me."

"No, thanks."

"Why? Are you a little flower of southern womanhood?" he asked me softly.

"A what? No!" I tried to hit him again, but this time he grabbed both my hands. "Let go," I said, laughing.

"Don't be afraid," he said.

"I'm not afraid!" My face was close to his. I looked into his eyes; then, impulsively, I leaned over and kissed him on the lips. He let go of my hands. "You asked for it," I said.

"No, no, it was nice. Do it again."

"Okay." Slowly I came forward and kissed him again. Then I sat back, feeling wonderful.

"Very good," Nathaniel said. He put his arm around my shoulders and pulled me close to him. Neither of us said anything as we stared at some people roller-skating around the fountain. A black guy in red tights was dipping and swirling in the white sunlight to music from a portable tape player.

But after a few minutes I thought about my dad. I got worried that he might be waiting for me back at the apartment. I touched Nathaniel's cheek. "I guess I should go back soon and see if my dad's home yet."

"You have to go?"

"Yeah, I think I'd better."

He pulled me forward and we kissed again. This time he moved his arms all the way around me and opened his mouth over mine. When we stopped kissing, I pressed my forehead against his. "I really have to go," I said.

"You really have to?" he said.

"Yes." I laughed.

"Can we finish this later?" he said.

"Okay," I whispered. I felt weak as we stood up and started across the park together. We passed a couple of the drug dealers, but they didn't bother us this time. The wind shook the trees; leafy shadows moved across the pavement.

Nathaniel and I stopped at the corner near my dad's apartment to say good-bye. "I'll call you tonight," he said. "Would you like to do something?"

"Sure. Maybe we could walk back to the park," I said.

"Yeah? And what will we do in the park?" he said.

I laughed breathlessly. "I don't know."

He kissed my forehead, then let me go. "I'll see you later," he said.

"Okay." I waved at him, then turned and hurried across the street to my dad's building.

21

Dad was home when I got in. He was stretched out on his bed and his eyes were closed. "Dad?" I said.

He didn't answer.

"Dad?"

His eyes opened. "What?" he said.

"Were you asleep?"

"Yeah, I, uh . . . I guess I was." He swung his legs over the side of the bed and sat up.

"No, go back to sleep," I said. "I'm sorry I woke you."

"No, no, that's okay. Where were you?" he said.

"Didn't you read my note? I just went for a walk."

"Oh, yeah. Right."

"Where had you gone?"

"Oh, I got restless and went out wandering." He rubbed his hands over his face.

"Is everything okay?" I said.

"Yeah, yeah."

"You look really tired. Don't you want to finish your nap?"

"No, no, let's go out. I don't want you to stay cooped up in this place."

"Oh, it's okay," I said. He looked so exhausted, I didn't want him to go out again just for my sake. "I'm really tired too. You can take a nap and I'll read or something."

"Well, maybe I will." He lay back on his bed and stared at the ceiling. "I didn't sleep last night."

"Why didn't you sleep?"

"Oh, I started thinking about things again. Wondering what the hell I was doing up here."

"You're doing what you should be doing," I said. "You're being creative."

"Yeah. . . . What would I do without you?" he said. He sighed and closed his eyes. "Don't leave me, bird," he said.

"Of course I won't." I sat on his bed and touched his knee. "You just need to rest," I said. "Then you can worry about all that stuff later. It'll be okay."

He smiled a little. "Thanks."

"You want me to close the shade?" I said.

"Please."

I went to the window and pulled down the shade.

"Thanks," he said. "Could you stay close by? You can read. There's a bunch of magazines on my shelves, and I got some stuff for sandwiches in the refrigerator."

"Great, I'll be fine. You just rest."

He closed his eyes again. "Okay, I'll rest," he said.

I got a few magazines and sat down at the kitchen table. I stared at my dad, wishing I could do more for him. I watched him until his breathing grew regular and his mouth dropped open a little. I felt like I was guarding over his sleep.

For the rest of the afternoon I sat at the table and read while Dad slept. I thought a lot about Nathaniel. I remembered how it felt to kiss him. When I turned the pages of the magazines, everything looked sort of wonderful. I thought all the clothes in the ads would look great on me, and ads for hotels and resorts—ads that had once made me feel lonely—now invited me and Nathaniel to stay in those places, swim in clear blue water, and dine by candlelight. One ad for British Airways showed a bridge silhouetted against a burnt-orange sky. I imagined me and Nathaniel together on that bridge, looking at that sky. I felt so excited, I had to get up a few times and pace around the apartment.

Around seven thirty I was making myself a sandwich when the telephone rang. I leaped across the room to grab it before it woke Dad up. "Hello?" I whispered.

"Hi. Why are you whispering?" Nathaniel said.

"Wait." I looked to make sure Dad was still sleeping. "Wait," I said again to Nathaniel, then I took the phone around the corner into the hall as far as the cord would reach. "Hi," I whispered. "My dad's sleeping."

"Well, what are *you* doing?" Nathaniel whispered.

"You don't have to whisper." I giggled. "I'm reading."

"Can you come out and play with me?" he said.

"I don't know." I was afraid to leave Dad, but I was dying to go out with Nathaniel.

"What's the matter? You have to take care of your dad?"

"No," I said. I knew I couldn't explain to him about guarding over Dad's sleep. "But he and I are going out in a little while."

"Oh. Well, in that case I guess I'll see you tomorrow."

"No—wait! Maybe we could get together for a few minutes," I said. "Before Dad and I go out, maybe I could meet you somewhere."

"Where?"

"Well, uh . . . do you know this little café called Maria's? They have a guitar player and a flute player."

"Sure," he said. "It's on Sixth Avenue. You want to meet me there?"

"Yes," I said. "We could meet there, then take a walk."

"Oh, yeah? Where would you like to walk to?" he said. His voice sounded sexy.

I giggled. "I don't know," I said. I pictured us stepping into an alley or a dark doorway to kiss.

"What time are you going out with Richard?" Nathaniel said.

"Oh, probably not before eight thirty. Maybe I could meet you there at eight."

"That doesn't give us much time," he said. "But I'll take it."

"Okay. I'll see you there at eight," I whispered.

We said good-bye and hung up. I went into my room and sat on my bed. I imagined what it would be like to hold Nathaniel again. I felt this strange combination of wanting to cry and needing to take deep gulps of air. I wished we could be together longer, but I was afraid my dad would get upset if I went out for more than a half hour. I hoped he'd still be sleeping and I could just leave him a note and say I'd gone to the store.

I pulled off my green T-shirt and tried on my white silk blouse. I changed into my jeans and my boots, then walked around my narrow little room to see how my outfit felt. My boots were too clunky, I thought. I took them off, put on my sandals, and walked around my room again. This time it was my jeans that didn't seem right—I could feel them brushing against my ankles. I took them off and pulled on my black silk skirt. As soon as I put it on, I felt wonderful—I couldn't believe I hadn't worn this skirt in the first place. I felt like a breeze in it. Silk was probably the perfect thing to wear when you hugged somebody, I thought.

I stepped lightly across the hall and into the bathroom. I pinned up my hair and put on fresh makeup, then I brushed my teeth. I only ran the water at the end so I wouldn't wake up my dad. I tiptoed back to my room and got out my grandmother's little black beaded purse to take with me: Then I wrote my dad a note saying I'd be back soon.

It was five to eight when I finally grabbed my purse, my keys, and my note and tiptoed out of my room. I stopped. Dad's eyes were open. "What are you doing?" he said.

"Oh . . ." I tried to smile at him, but it was hard. I was so disappointed to find him awake. "I'm going out for a little walk. I'll be right back."

"Please don't leave now."

"Why not?"

"I need you close by," he said.

"But Dad, I—I'm just going out for a few minutes," I said.

"I feel awful," he said, closing his eyes.

"Are you sick?"

"No. I don't know."

"You want me to go out and get you something? Some medicine or something?"

He shook his head. "No, I don't want you to leave," he said.

"I wouldn't be gone long," I said.

"I feel like I'm being buried alive," Dad said. "I can't even catch my breath."

I glanced at the clock. It was almost eight. If I wasn't at the café soon, Nathaniel would think I was standing him up. "Dad—"

"I'm so sorry," he said. He struggled to sit up.

"For what?"

"For everything I've done to you and Mackie. When I came to New York, I thought things would be different. I wanted to prove to Mackie that I could make it here."

"I know, Dad."

"But it's just as hard up here, Blue. In some ways

it's harder. I don't have the excuses I had in Layette."

I couldn't stand this. I hated seeing him this way, but I was afraid that if I said anything to comfort him, it would only prolong the conversation.

"I don't know why you've always believed in me," he said. "You always defended me. No matter what I did—if I forgot to pick you up from a friend's house or if I ignored you for days—you made excuses for me. You never deserted me. Why, Blue?"

I sat down at the table and stared at the plastic tablecloth. "Because I love you, Dad," I said quietly. I wished desperately he'd stop talking now.

"I've depended so much on you," he said. "Probably too much. Annie told me I had a false image of myself—that I think of myself as some misunderstood outsider. I've made you think that too, haven't I?"

I wasn't even listening to him. I didn't really care anymore what he was saying.

"Blue?"

"What?"

"Are you starting to see the truth? I'm not misunderstood. I'm just a loser with lots of excuses."

"I don't know, Dad," I said.

He lay back on his bed and stared at the ceiling without saying anything. After a little while he said, "I think you do know it. . . . It's okay. Now *I* have to face it. . . ."

I kept staring at the rooster design on the tablecloth and didn't say anything.

At about eight fifteen I glanced over at Dad. His

eyes were closed. "Dad, I'm going out for just a minute," I said. "I have to. Okay?"

He barely nodded. "Sure, babe. Thanks." I thought he was thanking me for staying and listening to him; it made me feel terrible, but it didn't stop me from wanting to escape the apartment. I stepped quickly to the door and let myself out.

I flew down to the street, then hurried around the corner to Sixth Avenue. It wasn't totally dark yet. The atmosphere on the street seemed festive; lots of people were out walking, and vendors were selling balloons and hot pretzels near the curb. I rushed through the crowd till I came to Maria's Café. I stepped in the front door and looked around at the nearly empty room. Nathaniel wasn't there. The clock over the bar said eight twenty. I went back to the patio. There was only a middle-aged man sitting out there reading the paper. The musicians weren't even playing tonight.

The waitress came by and asked me if I wanted a table. I mumbled, "No, thank you," then walked back out to the avenue. My fantasy of being with Nathaniel had been so strong that I could hardly accept that I'd missed him. I kept looking back over my shoulder as I walked home. Before I went upstairs, I stopped at a pay phone. I asked information for Annie's number, but when I called, there was no answer.

When I let myself into the apartment, Dad was still on the bed. He'd rolled over onto his side, and his back was to me. "Blue?"

"What?" I said.

"I'm glad you're back," he said.

I let out a puff of air and threw my keys down on the table. I started to head into my room.

"Bird, I want to talk to you about things," Dad said.

"No, Dad, not right now. I'm pretty tired," I said.

"Oh. Well, okay, babe," he said in a faint voice.

I stared at his back for a few seconds. I knew all I had to do was cross the room and sit on the floor beside his bed and start telling him the things I liked about him, tell him good things. But I didn't want to. "Good night," I said, and I went into my room.

22

I woke up to the muffled sound of someone sobbing. I turned on my lamp and looked at my watch. It was five thirty. I jumped out of bed and went into my dad's room. His lamp was on, and he was lying on his bed crying. He was still wearing his clothes from the night before.

I was scared as I walked over to the bed and said, "Dad?"

He struggled to sit up, covering his face with his hands. "I'm sorry, I can't stop this—" he said.

"What?"

"I can't—" He broke down again.

"Dad, what is it? What's wrong? Why are you crying?" I tried to pull his hands away from his face.

"Because it's hopeless," he said. He dried his eyes and looked at me.

"What's hopeless?" I said, kneeling in front of him.

"My life."

"No, it's not, Dad."

"Yes, it is." He looked down at his hands.

"No, Dad, it's not." I started to cry too.

"Nothing changes, ever," he said.

"Yes, it does," I sobbed. I clutched his arm.

He looked at me. "Blue, you're not listening to me. You're on automatic pilot. If I say no you say yes."

"What do you mean?"

"Listen. Just listen to me. I need to talk to you."

"Did I make you cry? I'm sorry about last night," I said.

"No, no. But I need you to listen," he pleaded. "I feel like I'm in this darkness and I just can't find a way out. It's like—it's like—you know why I don't drive a cab anymore?"

"Why?"

"Because I couldn't find my way around this city anymore. I was getting lost all the time. I'm lost in my head now, Blue. I'm trying to sort things out."

"I don't understand," I said.

"I know. I know you don't." He closed his eyes. "You agree with Mackie now, don't you?"

"No, I don't!" I was starting to feel desperate.

"Stop it, please!" he said. "Be honest with me. It's okay—I'm not going to get mad. I just want you to tell me the truth for a change."

"I do tell you the truth!"

"Oh, Blue . . ." He sounded angry.

"What's wrong?" I shouted.

"I'm sorry." He looked at me. "But you're not hearing me."

"I am too!" I shouted. I felt crazy. I felt like we'd

been trapped in this room having the same conversation for days.

"What I'm trying to say is that I need you to understand me—"

"I do understand you!"

He shook his head. "No, you don't."

"I do!"

"Would you just listen to me? Please?" He was almost shouting.

"I didn't do anything! Don't yell at me!" I covered my face.

"Just listen to me," he said.

"No!" I shrieked. "Leave me alone!"

He stared at me for a few seconds. "I'm sorry, babe," he said. "I messed up—I shouldn't have . . . I don't know what's wrong with me. I'm an idiot for badgering you like this." He went to his bureau. I thought he was going to put his money in his pockets, but suddenly he reached out and violently wiped all the coins and dollars off the top.

"Dad! Don't!" I stepped back into the hallway.

He picked up his brush and hurled it against the wall. He picked up the Faulkner books and threw them crashing to the floor, then he covered his face and wept.

"Stop! *Stop!*" I screamed.

He looked up at me. I was sobbing and shaking.

"Blue—" He stepped toward me, and I took a step back. "Don't—don't be afraid of me," he said.

I didn't say anything.

"I'm sorry, I'll leave you alone. I'm sorry. . . ."

He went to the door and opened it. "I'll—I'll leave you alone now," he said, and he left the apartment.

I didn't move for a few seconds as I stared at the closed door. Then I ran to the window and looked down at the street. I saw Dad heading toward the corner. "Dad!" I called out, but he didn't seem to hear me.

I ran into my room and pulled on my jeans and a sweater and my sneakers. Then I rushed out of the apartment and down the stairs. When I got to the stoop, I halted. The street was deserted. "Dad?" I called out.

I started down the sidewalk. It was still dark, and all the shops and restaurants were closed. A few cars rattled down the avenue. I ran to the corner and looked in both directions for Dad. I thought I saw his shadowy figure a couple of blocks down the street, walking away from me. "Dad!" I called, and I headed after him. When I got closer, he turned. It was a derelict in torn clothes. I let out a cry and ran back up the street. I thought I heard footsteps after me.

I ran around the corner and up the street to the next block. I turned that corner and kept running. Finally I looked over my shoulder and saw no one was chasing me. I stopped and tried to catch my breath. I didn't know where I was. I didn't recognize anything around me. I was terrified.

There was a truck parked at a newsstand a few blocks away, and some men were unloading bundles of newspapers. I started running to catch them before they drove away. I thought I could tell them my dad's address, and then maybe they could give me directions on how to get back there. But suddenly I stopped. I realized that I didn't have my keys with me. I couldn't get back inside the building now even if I did find it. I started to cry. I felt furious with my dad—he'd ruined my evening last night, and now it was his fault I was lost. Mom was right— he didn't know how to take care of me. I ran across the street, my sight blurred. I saw a phone booth near the newsstand and hurried toward it.

When I got inside the phone booth, I shut the door and dialed the operator. I told her I wanted to place a call to Layette, North Carolina. "Make it collect from Blue," I said. I felt calmer now that I was actually doing something. But when I heard my mother's familiar voice, I broke down crying again.

"Blue?" she said.

"Mom—I—"

"Blue, what's wrong?"

"Mom, I'm locked out of the apartment."

"Blue, what happened? Where's Richard?" she cried.

"He left! He went out, and then I followed him and I got lost, and now I'm locked out of the building!"

"Where are you?"

"I'm out on the street and it's all deserted, and I'm lost."

"Blue, I—I want you to call the police."

"What?"

"Call the police. Tell them your situation and have them come and get you."

"The police?"

"Do it, Blue," Mom said.

"Mom, I don't think I need to call the police," I said.

"Blue, don't argue with me now!"

I didn't say anything. I realized I'd just made a bad mistake.

"Blue?" Mom said. *"Blue?"*

"Mom, I don't want to go to the police station."

"Honey, you'll be safe there. Please, please do what I say."

"But, Mom . . ." I could hear her crying. "Okay, I will," I said.

"Call me when you get there," she said in a shaky voice.

"Okay . . . 'Bye, Mom." I hung up. I didn't know what to do. I couldn't go to the police station. If I did, I wasn't sure what would happen. Would my dad get in trouble? I stared at the street. It was starting to get light. A couple of joggers ran down the sidewalk, and a man in a business suit was hailing a cab nearby. Calling the police seemed silly. I stepped out of the phone booth. I wondered if I should ask the man in the suit how to get to my dad's address, and then I could just wait on the stoop till he came home. But the thought of waiting alone on the deserted street even in daylight frightened me. I stepped back into the phone booth. I watched the cab stop and pick up the man in the suit. As it drove away, I felt lonelier than ever. I thought of calling Nathaniel.

I picked up the phone again and called information for Annie Lawrence's number. I dialed, and on the second ring Annie answered with an alert-sounding "Hello?"

"It's . . ." I cleared my throat. "Blue Murray."

"Blue? What's wrong?"

"Is Nathaniel there?"

"He's sleeping. What is it, Blue? Is something wrong?"

"Yes, I'm locked out of my building," I said.

"Locked out? Where's Richard?"

"He—he went out for a walk."

"Where are you now, Blue?"

"I don't know," I said.

"Are you in the Village?"

"Yes, I think so—I'm not too far from the apartment, I don't think. It's just I'm not sure where I am exactly."

"Tell me the street names where you are. Look around and tell me the names of the streets."

"Okay." I looked at the sign on the corner. "Grove Street," I said.

"Grove Street and what?"

"I don't know. It doesn't say."

"Can you describe where you are? What are you near?"

"Well, I'm next to a bank, and across the street there's a newsstand in the middle of the intersection."

"Oh, sure, I know exactly where you are. You're very close to our apartment. Why don't you come over here, Blue? I think I might have a set of Richard's keys. Or if you like, you can wait here till he gets back home."

"Okay," I said. "But I have to call my mom. I talked to her a minute ago, and she wants me to go to the police station."

"The police station? That's sounds a little drastic, doesn't it?"

"Yeah, it does to me, too." I laughed a little.

"Well, come over here and we'll call her, okay?"

"Okay," I said.

Annie gave me directions and we hung up. Finally I felt like I was doing the right thing.

23

I found Annie's building and pressed the button next to her name in the vestibule. She buzzed me in, and I started up a narrow, fluorescent-lit staircase. I climbed five flights before I got to Annie's apartment. I knocked on the door and she opened it immediately. "Come in and catch your breath," she said.

Annie was wearing a white terry-cloth robe, and her hair was half pinned up, the other half falling down in frizzy curls. She looked paler and older than she had the other day in the restaurant. "I found a set of Richard's keys," she said, ushering me into her kitchen. "They're over there on the table."

"Thanks," I said.

Annie's kitchen had red brick walls and dark-green cabinets. There were no windows; a wall lamp over the table lit the room. I took Dad's keys from the table.

"Can I make you a cup of tea?" Annie said.

"Okay, but I better call my mother first," I said.

"Sure, the phone's over there on the wall," she said. "Call her, and I'll put the kettle on."

I had the operator put through a collect call to Mom's number, but the line was busy. I hung up. "It's busy," I said.

"Well, you can try again in a few minutes. Sit down," Annie said.

I sat at the table and watched her spoon loose tea into a pink teapot. Then she sat down across from me and lit a cigarette. "You know what?" she said, blowing out smoke. "I think my son's fallen in love with you."

I could feel myself blushing.

"I don't mean to embarrass you," she said, "but he was so happy when he came home after being with you yesterday that he spent three hours in the living room with the stereo headphones on, smiling the whole time."

"What was he listening to?"

She threw back her head and laughed. "I don't know," she said. "But I don't think that was the point."

The kettle started whistling. Annie jumped up and poured hot water into the teapot.

"Can I try my dad?" I said.

"Of course."

I got up and dialed Dad's number, but there was no answer. I could picture his empty apartment as I listened to the phone ring. I wondered if he was wandering around the city, weeping, feeling alone.

I hung up and sat back down. Annie set a cup of

tea in front of me. "Here's milk if you want it," she said, putting a carton of milk on the table. "And sugar." She moved the sugar bowl toward me.

I stirred some milk and sugar into my tea. I couldn't stop thinking about my dad. When I brought the cup to my lips, my hand was shaking. I put the cup down and rested my forehead in the palm of my hand.

"Blue?" Annie said.

"What?"

"Are you all right?"

I shook my head.

Annie was quiet for a few seconds, then she said, "Did something bad happen with Richard?"

"Yes."

"You want to talk about it?"

I stared down at the table. "Well, he left the apartment a little while ago. I don't know where he went. . . . I shouldn't have told my mother," I said.

"You can't protect him," Annie said.

"I know. But I shouldn't have told her."

"You don't think he can take care of himself?"

"No," I said, laughing a little.

Annie smiled. "He probably can. But I know how he gets. I worry about him too—you know that from the restaurant the other day."

I nodded.

"Was he depressed because his play didn't work out?"

"Yes. At first I didn't think he was that upset, but then he got very depressed."

"I know," Annie said. "He's fine at first, then he dwells on something till he's built up a big case against himself."

"Do you think something's really wrong with him?" I said.

"Well, he's a pretty unhappy person," Annie said. "I think he'd benefit a lot from therapy or something, but he doesn't want any part of it."

"My mom tried to get him to see a psychiatrist back home, but he wouldn't," I said.

"I know. I tried to get him to go to my therapist," Annie said. "But he got very angry about it. He's afraid, I think. We fought about it for a while. But that was about the time I decided I couldn't see him anymore."

"Why?"

"Well, I guess partly because of what I went through with Nathaniel's father. After we divorced, I decided I'd rather live alone than ever suffer like that again. I liked Richard a lot, but I didn't think I could help him, and he didn't seem to want to get help on his own."

"Do you think I could do anything to help him?" I said.

Annie stared at me. "I don't think so, Blue," she said.

We looked at each other for a moment, then tears came to my eyes. "Nothing?"

She shook her head. "You can love him, I guess."

I couldn't talk. Annie didn't say anything or make a move to bring an end to my crying. Finally I picked up a paper napkin from the table and wiped my eyes.

Then I took a deep breath and said, "I guess I should try calling my mother again."

"You want me to call her?" Annie asked.

"No, thanks. I better do it." I got up and placed another collect call to Mom. This time she answered.

"Hi, Mom," I said.

"Blue, where are you?"

"I'm at a friend's house. She's a friend of Dad's— her name's Annie."

"Blue, are you okay? I told you to go to the police!"

"But I'm safe here, Mom."

She sighed. "Honey, I want you to come home," she said.

"Come home? Mom, I want to stay with Dad longer."

"But you don't even know where he is! Listen—I know you're not going to like this, but I'm thinking of sending Uncle Walter up there to get you."

"Uncle Walter? No, Mom, don't!"

"Blue, I can't stand you being up there another minute."

"Mom, don't send Uncle Walter up here! He'll make everything worse!"

"Honey, I'm sorry, but I don't think I should have ever let you go up there alone."

"Oh, Mom, I wish I'd never called you! Dad just went out for a walk! He's fine! Please. I'm with two friends now—one of them is as old as you, so I'm safe here till Dad gets back. He didn't know I'd followed him. Please, Mom."

"Blue—"

"I'll have Dad call you as soon as he gets back and explain everything, okay, Mom?"

"I don't know . . ."

"It'll be okay. Just don't worry," I said. "Please, Mom, please . . ."

She didn't say anything for a few seconds.

"Well, I better go now, Mom. I'll talk to you later, okay?"

"Okay."

" 'Bye, Mom. Don't worry!"

"Blue—" She stopped and sighed. "Okay. 'Bye."

I hung up the phone. "Is everything all right now?" Annie said.

"I don't know. She was thinking of sending my uncle up here—"

Before I could say anything else, the door off the kitchen opened and Nathaniel stepped out of his room. He was wearing a pair of cutoffs and no shirt. His hair was tangled from sleeping.

"Hey—I thought I heard you out here," he said, staring at me. Suddenly I remembered about our broken date last night.

"Blue accidentally locked herself out of her building this morning," Annie said. "She called us and I told her to come over."

"Where's Richard?" Nathaniel asked quietly.

"I don't know," I said. I turned to Annie. "Do you know any place he usually likes to go?"

She shook her head. "Not really."

"I feel like I should look for him," I said.

"You want me to go with you?" Nathaniel said.

He sounded so serious. I wished I could quickly explain to him about last night.

"Don't you think it would be better if you just waited a little while?" Annie said. "I'm sure he'll come back."

"You want to look for him?" Nathaniel kept staring at me.

I nodded.

"Okay," he said. He went into his room and came out with his sneakers and a T-shirt. He put them on, then said, "I'm ready."

"Well, okay, 'bye, you two," Annie said. "Good luck."

" 'Bye, Mom." Nathaniel opened the door.

" 'Bye," I said to Annie. She was smiling at me. Her hair was really a wreck, but I liked the way she looked. "Thanks," I said, and I followed Nathaniel out into the hall.

Nathaniel led the way down the stairs to the street. He stopped on the sidewalk. "Where were you last night?" he said. He wasn't looking at me.

"Oh—I wanted to explain—I showed up, but you'd left," I said. "I was a little late."

"I waited until eight fifteen. I didn't think you were coming," he said.

"I'm sorry. My dad needed to talk to me."

"Oh." Nathaniel nodded and stared up the street. I felt uncomfortable. He wasn't being very friendly.

"What should we do?" I said.

"About your dad?" he said.

"Yes."

Nathaniel sighed. "Well, where do you think he went?"

"I don't know."

"Okay, well, let's try Sixth Avenue then," Nathaniel said.

It was light now, but the street outside Annie's building was still quiet. All the shops were closed; they had iron gates across their windows and doors. We turned a corner and passed the phone booth I'd called Mom and Annie from. Several people were buying papers at the newsstand. It seemed so safe. I couldn't believe I'd called my mother—I hated myself for betraying my dad.

"You want to head toward the park?" Nathaniel said, pointing.

"I don't know! I don't know where to go!" I almost started crying again.

"Hey, Blue—just relax. Your dad's going to be fine, okay?" He sounded impatient.

I turned away from him and stared at the sidewalk. I was embarrassed and angry that he'd told me to "relax."

"Well?" Nathaniel said after a few seconds.

"Well, what?" I said, my back to him.

"You want to cross the street?"

"Why not?" I still didn't look at him.

He touched my arm. "What's wrong?" he said.

"Nothing. I'm just relaxing," I said, moving away from him.

"Oh." He put his hands in his pockets. "Listen— I'm sure he's okay. Really," he said.

I just nodded, then started walking again.

Nathaniel stayed a couple of steps behind me. Neither of us talked. I could see the Empire State Building in the distance. More people were out on the sidewalks now, and cars rattled by us down the avenue. We'd never find my dad this way, I thought. The city seemed so big.

I stopped. "This is hopeless, isn't it?" I said, avoiding Nathaniel's eyes. "I think I should go back to Dad's place and wait for him there. He might even be there already."

"Okay, whatever you want," Nathaniel said. His voice sounded cold.

We started back the way we'd come. The few feet separating us now seemed like miles. When we got to my dad's building, I started to climb the steps to the front door, but Nathaniel stayed down on the sidewalk. I stopped. "Well," I said, "thanks for helping me look for him."

"Sure," he said, starting to back away. He wasn't even going to offer to come upstairs and wait with me.

"See you later," I said.

"Okay. 'Bye."

" 'Bye." I turned and hurried into the building.

When I unlocked the door to the apartment, I knew right away that Dad hadn't come back yet. The place felt totally empty. I threw myself down on the bed and pressed Dad's pillow against my face, finding relief in the darkness. I wanted to shut everything else out.

I stayed with my face in the pillow until my body relaxed and I fell asleep. I had bad dreams—I was aware even as I slept that everything was terrible; that my dad had disappeared, that my mother was scared and upset, that I'd had a terrible time with Nathaniel. I slept for a few hours. Every time I was close to waking, my dread pushed me back into sleep.

I didn't wake up completely until I heard the phone ringing. I sat up and grabbed the receiver.

"Blue?" Dad said.

"Dad, where are you?"

"Near the park."

"What are you doing there?" I cried.

"Calling you." His voice sounded tired and distant.

"Why are you calling me? Why don't you come home?"

"I didn't want to scare you."

"What do you mean?"

"I was afraid to barge in the apartment. I was afraid I might scare you because of the way I was acting this morning."

"I'm not scared of you," I said. "Come home."

"I would never hurt you," he said.

"I know that. Just come home!"

"Okay," he said after a pause.

"I'll wait for you downstairs!" I yelled. "Come right now! 'Bye!" I hung up the phone and hurried to the kitchen table and grabbed my keys; then I charged downstairs.

I sat on the front stoop and waited anxiously for Dad to appear. The late-morning sun had gone behind the clouds. It felt like it might start raining soon. I watched a man pulling a cart of balloon toys up the street. A mustard-colored mouse with black whiskers and a painted-on smile bobbed above all the other toys.

A cab honked. The driver stuck his head out the window and yelled at the balloon man to "Get the hell out of the street!" The balloon man pulled his cart over to the curb.

The cab wheeled around him and stopped a few doors down from our building. The back door opened and a large man dressed in a tan suit got out. He paid the driver, then turned around. I stared in horror at Uncle Walter's smooth, pink face.

"Hi, sugar," he said without smiling.

24

I stared at Uncle Walter. "You're here?" I said faintly.

"Your mother's hysterical about you, Blue," he said, walking toward the stoop. "You want to tell me what's been going on up here?"

I wanted to scream at him to go away, but I could hardly talk. I looked up the street, terrified my dad might appear any second. "I'm okay," I said. "Please, go home. Everything's all right now."

"Let's not get into a fight, sugar. I came up here to try and straighten things out. I think it would be best if you came back home with me."

"No!" I backed up a step, then yelled, "No! Please, go away!" I couldn't stand it if my dad found Walter here. He'd think I'd called and asked him to come take me home. "Leave us alone, please!" I shouted.

"Sugar—"

"You can't make me leave him!" I screamed. "He's my father."

A couple walked by and glanced up at me. Walter looked embarrassed. He stepped closer and spoke in a soft voice. "Sugar, I'm sorry, but we're all very worried about you," he said. "Your mother was crying when she called me this morning. Why do you want to keep hurting her like this?"

"I don't! I don't want her to be sad, but I need to stay here. Dad needs me to help him. I can't go now!"

"Okay, sugar, calm down." He looked past me toward the front door of the building. "Is your daddy home now?"

I looked wildly up the street, then back at Uncle Walter. I wanted to drag him away from the front of the building, pull him into an alley so my dad wouldn't see him when he rounded the corner.

"Please, please," I said. "Can you come back later? Can I at least talk to him first?"

"Why?"

"You'll upset him if he sees you now. He's not expecting you to be here."

Walter sighed and straightened up. "I think we've all done enough tiptoeing around Richard's delicate condition," he said. "That sort of nonsense went on too long before he left your mother, Blue. It's time we all started treating him like a grown man and not a little child."

"Don't talk about him that way!" I said.

"Oh, this is ridiculous," Walter said. "Excuse me." He moved past me up the steps.

"Wait!" I cried.

Walter stepped into the vestibule and buzzed my dad's apartment. After a moment he came back out onto the steps and looked at me. "Where is he, Blue?" he said.

"He's not home," I said. "Can't you just go somewhere and we'll come meet you later?"

"Well, that won't be necessary," Walter said, looking up the street. "Here he comes now." I turned and saw my dad coming toward us.

I tore down the steps and ran to him. "Dad!" I said, grabbing his arm. "Walter's here!"

"What?" He looked down the street, then looked back at me. "Why?" he said.

"Because I was scared this morning and I called Mom and she called him. They want me to come home, but I don't want to leave you!" I threw my arms around him.

"Okay, okay," he said, patting my back. He kept his arm around me and turned toward Walter. "Let's go talk to him," he said. We walked back to the steps together. "Hello, Walter," Dad said, nodding.

"Richard."

"What's up?" Dad said.

"I came here because Mackie got a call from Blue this morning. It sounded as if there were some serious problems up here." His voice was hard.

"Well, yes, we did have a little problem this morning," Dad said softly.

"A little problem? You run out on your daughter in the middle of the night—leave her locked out of your apartment, out on the streets all by herself—lost in the middle of New York City? Yes, I think you did have a little problem here."

"What?" Dad looked at me.

"I followed you," I said. "And I got lost—I forgot my keys."

"You *followed* me?"

I nodded.

"Oh, Blue." He rubbed his hand over his face and turned away from me.

"I came up here to take her home," Uncle Walter said.

Dad turned and stared at him for a few seconds. "Yeah . . . okay," he said quietly.

"Dad! I was just scared because I was locked out!"

"No, Blue," he said. "I think you should go back with him."

"*Why?* Why are you agreeing with him?" I said.

"Because I think it would be better for you."

"Why?"

"Because I'm not able to—" He glanced in Uncle Walter's direction. I knew it was hard for him to talk in front of Walter.

"But it's part my fault," I whispered furiously. "I didn't know what to say this morning!"

"No, no, no." He looked like he was in pain. "You didn't do anything wrong. I just can't keep using you."

"I don't know what you mean," I said. "Dad, please let me stay. I'm happy with you. Please let me." I hugged him.

He hugged me back. "No, you're not happy," he said softly. "You can't be happy—not when I'm miserable."

"I am happy," I sobbed. "I don't want to leave now."

"You can come back."

"When?"

"After I work some things out."

"Oh, Dad—"

He held me tightly for a moment, then turned to Uncle Walter. "It's okay. She can go back with you," he said. "But I'd like a little time to talk to her alone. Do you have a flight booked?"

Uncle Walter looked at his watch. "Well, I guess we could spare an hour," he said. "I'll meet y'all back here at about one thirty, how'd that be?"

"Thanks," Dad said. "And, uh, thanks for being concerned enough to come all the way up here."

Uncle Walter nodded. "It's okay, Richard," he said. Then he headed up the street. We both watched him till he turned the corner.

"You want to go upstairs?" Dad said.

I nodded.

"Come on." He put his hand against my back and we walked up to the front door together.

When we got inside the apartment, Dad said, "I think I need a cup of coffee first. You want one?"

"No, thanks."

While Dad was making his coffee, I went into my room and sat down on my cot. I stared at my clothes, stacked in neat piles beside the bed. I couldn't believe I was going home today.

I heard the kettle whistling and Dad moving around in the kitchen. I pictured him alone in this apartment after I'd gone. I buried my face in the pillow he'd bought me. This was a nightmare.

"Bluebird?" Dad said. I looked up. He was standing in the doorway, holding his cup of coffee. "Are you okay?"

"No. I'm terrible." I looked away from him. "If I leave now, then everything's been a failure."

Dad walked over and sat down beside me. He put his coffee cup down on the floor and took my hands. "Listen," he said. "I want to tell you some things."

"What?"

"I walked all over this city this morning, thinking about you and me and about my life and your life. . . . I've done some bad things to you—"

"No, you—"

"Listen," he said. "I love you more than anything else in the world. The hardest thing I've ever had to do was drive out of the driveway last February with you crying and yelling in the yard. I cried all the way to Richmond. And then this morning I made you cry again—God, I even had you running out into the streets trying to look after me."

"But—" I said.

He held up his hand. "It's crazy, Blue. I want you to be happy—I don't want to keep making you miserable."

"But I want to stay here and help you," I said.

"No. You can't help me by being here. I have to work some things out on my own. The best way you can help me now is by being happy in Layette. I want you to have good things." He squeezed my hands. *"I don't want to make you cry anymore,"* he said.

"But what will happen to you?" I said.

"I'll be fine. I'll get some help. I promise. Really.
. . ." He looked me in the eyes. "Really. Don't worry
about me, okay?"

I felt like he was asking me to do the hardest thing
of all—to go home and try to be happy without him.
"I don't know if I can," I said.

"You have to, Blue," he said. "Or I won't make
it. If I keep hurting you, I won't make it. I'll hate
myself too much."

I realized then what a brave thing he was doing,
letting me go and asking me to be happy and not
worry about him. "Okay," I said. "I won't worry
about you."

He stared at me for a moment. "Thanks," he said
softly. He sighed, then he looked around the room.
"Well, I guess we should get your stuff packed." He
looked at his watch. "Then we'll have some time.
What would you like to do?"

"I don't know," I said. "I guess we could take a
walk."

He nodded. "That'd be nice," he said; then he
stood up.

"I better call Nathaniel," I said. "He was helping
me look for you this morning."

"Oh, yeah?" Dad stared at me for a couple of seconds. "Do you want to see him before you go?"

I was amazed he was offering to take me to see
Nathaniel in our last hour together. "You think we
could?" I said.

"Yeah, I think we could," he said. "Why don't you see if he's home?" He stepped into the hall. "I'm going to take a quick shower."

"Okay," I said. Dad went into the bathroom and I went into his room and dialed Nathaniel's number. Annie answered. "Hi, Annie," I said. "It's Blue."

"Oh, Blue! Did Richard come home?"

"Yes," I said.

"Is everything all right?"

"Well, not really. I have to go back to North Carolina," I said. "My uncle came up here."

"Oh, no!" Annie said. "That's rotten! When are you leaving?"

"In about forty-five minutes. Is Nathaniel there?"

"No, he's gone out to do a couple of errands, then he was going to stop by the restaurant. I'm on my way there now. I'll tell him to call you."

"That's okay," I said. "Maybe we could stop by so I can say good-bye to him."

"Oh, that's great!" Annie said. "Then I can say good-bye to you too."

"Oh, yeah, both of you. Well . . . I guess we'll be over there soon."

"Is Richard coming with you?"

"Yes," I said.

"Oh, I'm glad," she said. "I'll see you guys there."

We hung up and I went into my room to pack. I threw all my things into my bags, except my black silk skirt and white silk blouse. I put them on, then pinned up my hair. When my dad came out of the bathroom, I was standing in the kitchen ready to go.

"You look wonderful," he said as he dried his hair. He was wearing a pair of dark pants and a plaid shirt.

"Thanks," I said.

He went over to his bureau and put his change in his pocket and combed his hair. I watched him sit down on his bed and pull on a pair of black socks and his black loafers. "Ready?" he said.

I nodded.

For a couple of seconds, his face looked terribly sad, but then he stood up and said, "Okay, bluebird." He walked to me, put his hand on my shoulder, and guided me out of the apartment.

25

It was gray and humid as we headed to Bleecker Street. "I like Annie's restaurant," I said.

"Oh, have you been there before?" Dad said.

I nodded. "Day before yesterday Nathaniel took me there after the movies," I said.

"No kidding? You've gotten around, haven't you?"

"Yeah."

"Nat's a nice kid," Dad said.

"I know," I said.

We turned the corner and walked to the white brick building with the green awning. I looked in the front window and saw Nathaniel sitting at the bar. "Oh—he's in there," I said nervously.

"Good," Dad said.

When we entered the restaurant, Nathaniel turned around and smiled at me. I decided I didn't even have to apologize for this morning—he looked really glad to see me.

"Hi, Nat," Dad said.

"Hi, Richard," Nathaniel said.

"How you doing, Doug?" Dad said, and he went to the far end of the bar and started talking to Doug. I knew he was trying to give me and Nathaniel a little privacy.

I went over to Nathaniel and sat down on the stool beside him. "Hi," I said.

"Hi. Mom told me you were leaving today."

"Yeah, my uncle came up here to get me. I just came over to say good-bye."

He took my hand. "When are you coming back to visit me?" he said.

"I don't know."

"Well then, maybe I'll come down to North Carolina and visit you. I have some money saved," Nathaniel said. Then he drawled, "I'd enjoy a trip to the deep South." He did a terrible imitation of a southern accent.

"Not if you talk like that," I said.

He laughed and squeezed my hand.

The door in the back swung open and Annie came out of the kitchen. "Hi, Blue," she said. "I'm sorry you have to leave today."

"Me too," I said.

"I hope you can come back sometime."

I nodded. She smiled at me, then she glanced over at my dad. "Hey—it's really good to see you," she said.

"It's good to see you, too," he said. Annie left me and Nathaniel and went to the other end of the bar to talk to Dad.

Nathaniel tugged on my hand. "You going to write me?" he said.

"Yes."

"Long letters?"

"Yes."

"Good. I'll write you back," he said.

"You better," I said. "You really should come visit me in Layette. We have lots of room."

"Oh yeah? That doesn't matter," he said close to my ear. "We only need one room."

"Is that so?" I said, feeling a shiver go through me.

"We just came over so Blue could say good-bye," I heard Dad say to Annie. "I guess we better get back to her uncle now."

"Well, come back sometime," Annie said. "I've missed you."

Dad nodded at her then headed to the door.

"Good-bye, Blue." Annie waved at me.

I waved back at her and stepped away from Nathaniel. "See you," I said to him.

" 'Bye," he said.

Dad opened the door. I held Nathaniel's gaze for a few seconds then turned and joined Dad outside under the green awning.

We started walking. We walked sadly without talking. When we turned off Bleecker Street, I could see Uncle Walter in the distance waiting on the stoop. I felt a raindrop hit my arm and another hit my hair. I stopped and grabbed my dad's arm. "It's raining," I said in a voice full of tears.

"I know," Dad said.

"I don't know how I'll say good-bye to you without crying!" I said, my voice rising.

"Let's not say good-bye when you leave," he said.

"Well then, don't say you love me either," I said. "And don't call me bluebird. They'll both make me cry."

"Okay. I won't," he said. He took my hand and held it tightly as we headed toward Uncle Walter.

When we reached the building, Dad and Uncle Walter and I went up to the apartment. The two of them waited in silence while I got my things. When we got to the downstairs hall, the rain outside was coming down hard. "I'll get a cab," Dad said.

"Thanks, Richard," Uncle Walter said.

I watched through the glass door as Dad ran down the steps, hunching his shoulders against the rain. He ran to the corner and hailed a cab, then ran alongside it back down our street. When it stopped in front of our building, he opened the door and motioned for me and Uncle Walter to come. We picked up my things and stumbled out into the rain.

"Good-bye, Richard," Uncle Walter said, and he got into the back of the cab.

Dad and I stood close to each other, looking at each other's faces as the rain pelted our heads. Then he kissed my forehead and I quickly ducked down into the cab. As we pulled away, I watched him through the rain-streaked back window, my heart breaking because he was getting so wet. I wanted him to go inside and get dry, but he kept standing there as we drove away.

Uncle Walter called Mom from La Guardia Airport to let her know we were on our way home. On our flight we were both quiet. He seemed to understand that I didn't feel like talking. When our plane landed in Raleigh, he got his car out of the airport parking lot and drove me to our house.

It was late afternoon when the tires of Walter's Buick crunched over our pebble drive. Mom was waiting in one of the rockers on the front porch. She stood up and walked down the steps to the driveway.

I got out of the car and looked at her. "Hi," I said.

"Hi, honey," she said.

"I'm going in," I said, and I carried my bags past her up the steps. I went into the house, leaving her and Uncle Walter to talk on the porch.

I dropped my stuff in the front hall and walked back to the TV room. I sat on the couch and stared at the room as if I were seeing it for the first time. Everything looked so clean and pretty—the shiny parquet floors, the pastel curtains, the light-wood furniture.

I could hear Uncle Walter talking to Mom on the porch, but I couldn't make out what he was saying. Other sounds came from outside—children yelling as they played in the yard across the street; the magnolia leaves scraping against the window screen behind the sofa. I had to live in this house in this town now without dreaming about my dad and New York City all the time. I sat back and closed my eyes.

I heard Uncle Walter's car start up and drive out of the driveway. I didn't want to face Mom now. Too much had happened and I didn't know what to say to her. I turned and looked out the window.

I heard her walk through the living room.

"Oh. There you are," she said.

I didn't turn around.

"Hey, you," she said.

I didn't answer. After a moment I thought I heard her sniff. I turned to look at her. She stood in the shadowy light with her hands covering her face.

"What's wrong?" I said.

She sniffed again and wiped her eyes. "I'm sorry you had to come home today," she said.

"Is that why you're crying?" I said.

She nodded.

"Did you want more of a vacation from me?" I said, trying to make a little joke.

She shook her head and sat down on the couch next to me. "No. I wanted you to be close to Dad and"—her voice broke—"and I wanted him to be happy."

"I think he's going to get happier," I said.

She stared at me. "You think so, Blue?"

"He promised me he was going to get help," I said.

"You think he will?" She looked at me earnestly, as if she really wanted to believe me.

"Yes," I said, though the truth was I didn't really know for sure what would happen to him now.

Mom let out a long shaky sigh and stared at the floor. I reached over and patted her back. Neither of us talked for a while. A warm breeze blew through the window. A screen door slammed across the street, and someone started calling the children to come inside.

About the Author

Mary Pope Osborne was born in Fort Sill, Oklahoma, and graduated from the University of North Carolina at Chapel Hill.

She is the author of a previous novel for young adults, *Run, Run, As Fast As You Can*, that was hailed by the critics when it was published in spring 1982.

Ms. Osborne currently lives in Greenwich Village, New York City, with her husband, Will, and is at work on her third novel.